I0587985

ALSO BY ELIZABETH BONESTEEL

SURVIVAL TACTICS

A SHORT STORY COLLECTION BY

ELIZABETH
BONESTEEL

REVISED AND EXPANDED EDITION

HOUSE
PANTHER
PUBLISHING

CONTENTS

INTRODUCTION TO THE SECOND EDITION

I don't expect anyone to actually believe this, but I came up with the title for this collection before lockdown. But it kind of works, doesn't it? I never in my life leaned on art as much as I have over the last eighteen months, and I know I'm not alone.

This expanded edition includes all the stories from the first edition, plus three. "Unto Dust," a Central Corps tie-in story, came out last year and was briefly up on my web site. The other two—"The Haunting of Jessica Lockwood" (another Central Corps tie-in) and "Birthdays at the End of Time"—are new for this book.

One other change: I've added a content warnings page. The page is at the end of the book, to avoid the inevitable spoilers, but if there are particular issues you'd like to be warned about, it's there as a reference. I've tried to be both nuanced and thorough, but I am certain to have missed things here and there, for which I apologize.

The world is a mess right now. Let's give each other nice things.

INTRODUCTION

Most of the stories in this collection were written during a particularly fraught time in my life. Their content reflects this. While there's optimism (and, of course, a little romance), there's also despair, and a lot of anger. Some of it's expressed pretty graphically—turns out short stories make terrific therapy.

Tonally this collection is all over the map, but modulo language, only three stories merit traditional content warnings. These are "About Time," which includes suicidal ideation; "Single Point of Failure," which includes suicidal ideation and some graphic violence; and "Thinking Inside the Box," which includes violence and sexual abuse.

I will say that with one exception (well, maybe two, depending on how you look at it), all of these stories end on a positive note. Rage only becomes despair if you give up.

ABOUT TIME

For Gerald

1.

"Excuse me," Nora asked the woman in the long coat, "do you have the time?"

Stupid question, she thought, even as the woman startled, turning away from the train tracks she'd been staring at with disconcerting intensity. But it was the only question Nora'd been able to think of: the subway clock, an ancient bright-red digital display, had stopped working again, and it gave Nora the excuse.

Nora might have left the woman alone otherwise. Despite the fact she'd watched the woman—Nora's own age, more or less, but so much more poised and elegant—every weekday morning for nearly a year, there was no reason for Nora to believe there was anything alarming about the way she was looking down at the electrified rails, her expression almost wistful.

There was no wistfulness in the glare she gave Nora. She

flicked her eyes toward the broken clock, and resignation took over her face. "Sure," she said, her accent marking her as a local. She dropped her right hand into one deep pocket and pulled out her phone. "8:24." She turned away again.

"Thanks," Nora said. From the tunnel she heard the squeal of a train coming around the too-tight corner into the station; it would be the E line, the one the woman in the long coat climbed on every morning. Around her, people began to shuffle forward, raising their voices to be heard over the sound of the incoming engine. "Wait," Nora added, wondering where her newfound bravery had come from. "Are you—is everything all right?"

She wasn't sure, at first, that the woman in the long coat had heard her. But then she turned, and the glare was sharper, and she said, "Mind your own business." And the crowd swept her away.

Nora kept her eyes on the train until it rounded the corner out of sight, and the station fell back into relative quiet, the only sounds the hissing of the HVAC and the hum of the electric transformers. Around her, people stood in pairs and groups, heads together, talking quietly. Nora stood alone.

She turned back, and out of the corner of her eye she saw the broken clock flash. Not numbers, oddly enough, but letters: TY.

Some kind of error code, she thought. When she blinked, it was displaying the time again.

Nora decided she would stop looking for the woman in the long coat, but the next day the woman found her.

"Listen," she said. Her hair, shaved away from one side of her head and hanging long over the other, had fallen into her eyes; absently she swept it behind her ear. "I'm sorry. Yesterday. I was rude."

She wasn't glaring, but she wasn't looking at Nora, either, instead staring somewhere over Nora's shoulder. Her skin was warm brown, touched with gold, and Nora couldn't tell if she was blushing, but something in the woman's face suggested she was embarrassed.

"You weren't rude," Nora told her. "I interrupted."

"That old clock though." At last the woman met Nora's eyes, this time with a self-conscious smile. "You'd think they'd replace it."

"They figure we all get the time on our phones," Nora said.

"You don't have a phone."

Nora did have a phone. Like everyone else's, its lock screen displayed the time. She hadn't thought about it, watching the woman stare at the train tracks. "It was at the bottom of my pack," she lied, gesturing at her overstuffed bag. "But I shouldn't have bothered you."

"It's okay," the woman said. "It's just the time."

The E train pulled up; Nora hadn't even noticed the noise.

"That's my train," the woman said. Then: "Okay. Well, bye."

She turned and walked toward the edge of the platform, and Nora felt the familiar push of the crowd around her. She stumbled, and instinctively glanced at the clock to check on her own train.

Except this time the clock said NAME.

Nora blinked. The word remained.

"Oh!" She turned back to where the woman was receding into the crowd. "Hey," she called. "Hey. I'm Nora."

The half-shorn head stopped and turned back in her direction. The woman said something, and Nora saw her smile, and she disappeared on to the train car.

She must have heard wrong. That wasn't a name.

When Nora glanced back at the clock, it said ELSE.

"But that's *not a name*," she told it.

A moment later, the clock blinked again, and said 8:26.

When Nora next saw the woman in the long coat, she was carrying two paper cups of coffee.

"I took a chance," she said, approaching Nora with that same shy smile. She held out a cup.

Nora, who made cheap coffee in her apartment with the expensive coffee maker her old boyfriend had left behind, took the cup and gently pried off the lid. The smell was rich and strong, the coffee pale. She took a sip, glancing at the woman's cup; scrawled on the side in coffee-shop Sharpie was the word ELSE.

"So that *is* your name," she said.

The woman grimaced. "It's a nickname. My real name's worse."

"As bad as Nora?"

"Nora's sweet."

Nora felt mildly giddy. "It's old-fashioned."

"You want to hear old-fashioned? My whole name's Elspbeth."

Nora thought the name was beautiful, but something in Else's voice made her laugh. "It's very Victorian."

"To go with my very Victorian image."

She was funny. Else was funny.

"My mother says she gave me the name because she wanted me to be an old-fashioned girl. I started calling myself Else because—"

"—you wanted to be called something else."

Nora bit her tongue; she shouldn't have interrupted. But this time Else was laughing. "Anything else, really. That's how I sign my artwork: A.E. Silva."

"You're an artist."

"You haven't heard of me?"

Nora blinked. "I'm not much in touch with the art world," she said.

Else shrugged. "Wouldn't matter if you were. Nobody's heard

of me." She looked away, and some of the light had gone out of her eyes. "What do you do?"

"Software," Nora told her. How could she make Else smile again?

"Really?" Else turned back, interest in those eyes. "I'd heard it was awful there. For women. You hear all these stories."

"It is awful, in some places," Nora allowed. "But I like it."

"Why?"

Nora couldn't remember ever being asked that before. "It's fun. It's like—did you ever do puzzles as a kid? Like Sudoku? Or logic puzzles?"

"You mean 'Jerry is three inches taller than the boy in the blue vest' kinds of things?" Nora waited for ridicule, but instead Else said, "I used to love those."

"It's like that," Nora told her. "Like doing logic puzzles all day."

"And you never got shit for being a woman?"

Nora became abruptly aware of the crowd, and the time. She glanced at the clock. 8:27 and still no train. She blinked her eyes, and the clock said LATE. And then, a moment before switching back to the time: TALK.

"When I started," she said, "I was late for this meeting. When I got to the room I heard everybody joking and laughing, but when I walked in they all went silent. Just stared at me while I sat down. After that, they were all really stiff, until this one guy—Tamal—he was arguing a design point, and he said the manager's idea was bullshit. Everybody looked scandalized, but they were staring at *me*. And I realized they were worried about swearing in front of the girl."

Else gasped. "What did you do?"

"I told them I thought the manager's idea was bullshit, too."

The screech of the train drowned out Else's response, but she was laughing again, and Nora decided her exact words didn't matter that much. "Sorry," Else shouted above the noise. "Gotta go. See you tomorrow!"

Nora raised her coffee in lieu of a farewell, and Else waved, rushing into her train car. Nora watched the car pull out of the station and disappear down the tunnel, and she stared at the darkness for a full minute.

"You could have delayed it a bit longer, you know," she said aloud.

When she turned to the clock, it was saying: SRRY.

2.

"Do you believe in ghosts?" Nora asked Else.

They were sitting in the coffee shop before 8:00 am. Throughout high school and college, Nora had sworn she'd never take any job that required her to be coherent that early. Else was shattering all her habits.

"You mean like apparitions?" Else asked. "Clouds in the corner? Your grandma watching you have sex? That kind of thing?"

Nora could feel herself blushing. "More like lights flashing when they're not supposed to."

"Ah." Else sat back, all authority. "You mean a poltergeist."

"Like the movie?" Nora frowned. "They were nasty in that movie."

"Not at the beginning."

Nora thought of the clock, and the train delay. "No, it doesn't make sense."

"Are you haunted, Nora?"

Else was laughing again, but when Nora said, "I don't know," she stopped.

"You need to not listen to spirits, Nora," she said, all seriousness. "Voices in your head? They lie."

There was something in her voice, something inviting Nora to ask and not to ask all at once. Nora opened her mouth to tell Else the truth, then smiled. "No voices in my head," she said. "Just— coincidences sometimes look like more than that, you know?"

SRRY, she thought at the clock.

The internet told Nora that poltergeists didn't haunt locations, but people. In her small apartment one Friday night, facing two days without Else, she turned off all the lights and said, "Are you here?"

There was nothing.

The train station Nora waited at every morning was one of the oldest in the country. In more than a hundred years, a hundred and twelve people had died at the station. Thirty-two had died on the tracks.

Tracking down all the obituaries was problematic, even for the internet, and Nora discovered there were still such things as librarians. This one, a woman Nora's mother's age, didn't even blink at the morbid request.

"Most of the microfilm has been digitized," she said. "I'll log you in and let you do a search. But anything before 1938 or so is going to be a physical archive. Having the dates will help."

Nora made notes of names, ages, and modes of death, and learned more than she wished about what a train could do to a body, no matter how hard the conductor slammed on the brakes. But the one that struck her most was not a death on the tracks. It was a footnote, a small boxed obituary on the front page of a now-defunct newspaper dated 1933:

LOCAL MAN DIES OF HEAD INJURY

*Gerald Newby, aged 33, of Beacon Street, died yesterday a#er
striking his head on a concrete pi$ar at Park Street Station. Mr.
Newby was employed at Goorin Bros. Hat Shop on Salem Street.
He is survived by his mother, Ruth, and his sister, Elspbeth.*

Nora felt a chill up her spine.

"Thank you," she told the librarian. "I've found what I want!
ed." She tried not to rush too obviously as she helped the woman
put the materials away.

She got up early on Sunday, long before the Saturday night
revelers would be awake enough to frequent the trains. Even so,
the station was milling with people, and she had to adapt her original plan of shouting up at the clock.

I didn't have to shout before, she thought.

She put her arm around a cement pillar and leaned against it,
trying to look as if she were waiting for a train. "Mr. Newby?" she
asked. "Gerald? Is it you?"

The clock was half-heartedly draped in plastic, its face dark.

After nearly a minute, it said: YES

Every hair on Nora's body stood on end. "Are you a
poltergeist?"

NO

"Are you stuck here?"

The clock was dark for a long time.

YES

"Oh." Nora had to blink. "I'm sorry, Gerald."

SOK

"Do you like it here?"

LTTL

That one took her a moment. "A little?"

YES

"What do you like?"

PPL

It would be, she realized, the perfect location: crowd after crowd, over years and decades. Birth and death would change faces, but not the fact of the company. Gerald could watch as much as he liked.

But that was very nearly all.

"Do you talk to a lot of people?"

NO

"Why me?"

HELP

"You wanted to help me?"

NO

"I'm sorry; I don't understand. Why me, then?"

HELP

She didn't know how to break down the line of questioning any better. "Is there anything I can get you, Gerald?"

NO

TY

"You're welcome."

She stood there for a while, watching the crowd grow as the city woke up. Eventually, she said, "I have to go now, Gerald."

OK

"Gerald. Are you lonely?"

There was another long pause before the clock replied.

NOT

NYMR

For the rest of the day, Nora felt light.

3.

The next day, Else didn't show up at the coffee shop.

When she was missing again on Tuesday, Nora called in sick to work and went back home. She'd avoided internet searches before, not wanting to feel like a stalker; but worry drove all of that out of her head.

A.E. Silva, she typed in the browser search bar.

The first page of results were all images, and she realized she'd never asked Else what sort of art she made.

They were sculptures, all iridescent glass and impossible colors, graceful and fluid like the lines of Else's coat. Abstracts, every one, although Else had given them names: *More Laughter*, one was called; another, *Passion Tears*. Nora stared at them, each one a perfect transcription of a part of Else's personality, happy and sad and frivolous and serious all at once.

There was one in greens and blues, curved over itself in impossible balance, that reminded Nora of the look she'd seen on Else's face that first day, when she'd been staring at the train tracks. The sculpture should have toppled under its own weight, and indeed it looked as if it would at any moment.

Failure, it was called.

Nora entered her credit card number into a public records site, and came up with an address a few blocks away from their coffee shop. So close. All along Else had been so close. For years, maybe.

Nora dialed the number as she headed out the door. Else didn't answer.

Nora leaned on Else's buzzer until she heard the intercom click. "Get the fuck off my doorbell," Else said, and Nora nearly passed out from relief.

"It's me," she said.

There was a long silence. Nora wished for Gerald, and then there was a click as the door unlocked.

The building was short—six stories without an elevator—and Else lived on the top floor. By the time she arrived, Nora was puffing; but Else opened the door at her step.

She looked as if she hadn't bathed in several days; her long hair was matted and sticking up at angles from her face.

"Well," Else said. "I suppose you should come inside."

Else's one large room sported crown moulding and wide wood floors, and a single countertop kitchen. Beyond that, there was a mattress on the floor and a laptop sitting next to it. Cushions were scattered against the walls. Nora wondered if this was some sort of artists' lifestyle.

"I was worried," she said.

Else turned away and shuffled to the counter. "I'm sorry," she said, and her voice was gray. "I have bad days sometimes. Do you, Nora?"

Not like this. "How can I help?" she asked.

Else had pulled two mugs out of the cabinet and was pouring coffee. Not as rich as the coffee shop's, but from the smell Nora thought it was from the same beans. "I think," Else said, "I just need to get through it."

Nora took the cup Else offered her.

Nora was not a taker of risks; she never had been. Software was not her dream profession, but she'd had an aptitude, and it paid enough. Before Else, she'd been gliding through life, comfortable if not joyous, safe if not secure. Her handful of relationships had each petered out due to apathy on both sides; she was fairly certain she'd never had her heart broken. All the songs, after all, said she would know.

She was not a taker of risks. But she said: "Do you want company?"

And Else smiled.

"I should go home," Nora said.

"No."

They were curled around each other on the mattress on the floor, the remains of three take-out meals around them, no lighting but the glow from the laptop screen. Nora had thought she understood contentment, but she'd never felt anything like this soul-deep wholeness.

"I should have cooked for you. I'm a lousy guest."

"You're terrible. Stay."

"I didn't come for this. I came to cheer you up."

Else lifted her head off Nora's shoulder and looked into her eyes. In the half-dark Else was luminous, like an apparition, and Nora tightened her arms around her.

"You did cheer me up," Else told her.

For a long time, they didn't talk.

Before dawn, they got up and showered. Nora fluffed out her short curls, and then with a wide-toothed comb tugged the tangles out of Else's long, wet hair.

"The day we met," Else told her, "when you asked me for the time." She inhaled. "Nora. I was staring at the train tracks."

"I know," Nora told her.

"I would have, if you hadn't stopped me."

"I know."

"Why did you stop me?"

"Someone was looking after us," she said.

"Call me the second you get home," Else commanded as Nora left.

The morning was clear and cold, the air full of the sharp, tangy city smells that Nora loved. So beautiful here, the sprawling buildings, some reaching high into the clouds; the green spaces; the gridded streets and the wandering paths. More people than Nora could count smiled at her, and she didn't wonder, because she knew somehow she was glowing, the fire inside of her visible through her skin, blazing the world around her with joy.

She took the stairs down to the train station, only to find two workmen setting up a scaffolding under the clock.

"What are you doing?" she asked.

They each gave her a quick, assessing glance, then turned back to their work. "Replacing it," they told her. "Took long enough for them to cough up the cash."

Nora found her cement pole. "Gerald," she said, "will you be all right?"

YES

If the men taking the clock down saw the word, they didn't react.

"Can I do anything?"

NO

"But you're stuck in the clock, aren't you?"

NO

Oh. "You're stuck at the station."

YES

"So I'll see you again."

A long pause.

DONT

KNOW

Something tightened in her chest. "Gerald. I want—before, when you said HELP. You didn't mean you were helping me, did you?"

NO

And then:

ELSE

"You knew what she was going to do."

YES

"You've seen it."

YES

Her vision was growing blurry. "You saved her life."

NO

YOU

"I love her."

GOOD

HPPY

BE

HPPY

NORA

"Obsolete piece of crap," one of the workmen remarked, and yanked the wires out of the ceiling.

4.

"Else. You're not ready."

"What? Of course I am."

Nora frowned at her. "You've been painting. There's color in your hair. The non-premeditated kind."

Else had dyed her long hair bright blue three weeks earlier, but the yellow blob of paint clinging to the tips was not part of her planned look. Else looked down, swore, and headed back to the bathroom. "I shouldn't have worn white," she groused.

Else looked beautiful in white. She looked beautiful in everything.

Nora had asked Tamal what they ought to wear when he'd invited her and Else to be his son's godparents. She had never seen him in anything other than jeans and a polo shirt, and he'd laughed at her. "Be there. Bring love. The rest is up to you."

At Else's suggestion, Nora was in pale blue. "Because you're the sky," Else had told her, shyly. "Always there, no matter how cloudy I get."

Else emerged from the bathroom, hair cleaned, and picked up their coffee mugs. "Can we get breakfast after?" she asked, heading for the kitchen.

"Sure. But please, real food. If I have more donuts my brain will short-circuit."

"There's no such thing as too many donuts." Else poured out the now-cold coffee and ran water into the mugs. "You ready?"

"Been ready for ten minutes. C'mon."

Else pulled on her long coat, and something about the way the garment flowed over her dress made her look like royalty. Nora didn't realize she was grinning like a fool until Else waved a hand before her eyes. "Nora. We'll be late."

Nora grabbed her own coat off the hook by the door. "There's a brunch place around the corner from the church," she said.

Else made a face. "I hate brunch." She opened the door. "Bye, Gerald," she said over her shoulder.

"Bye, Gerald," Nora echoed.

Before she pulled the apartment door shut behind her, Nora saw the coffee maker flash

BYE

FACTORY RESET

D*EFINITION:* Felis lutrina. *Indigenous pentapedal pseudomammalian carnivore. Diet based on smaller mammals, rodents, and insects. No plant-based consumption in evidence. Hunts in groups and will attack larger prey. Rudimentary problem-solving skills; no recorded tool use. Colloq. were-kat.*

ADDENDUM: In groups of three or more, capable of killing and consuming humans. Treat with extreme caution. All we found of Raffiq were fingernails and teeth.

SALVAGE REPORT
Haven Systems Terraformer Model 8
(deactivated)

Day One

Followed all day by a pack of *felis lutrinae*—seven or eight of them, I'm not sure. Despite the aggression documented by the original terraformer installation team, their behavior suggested little more than mild curiosity. They wove in and out of the deeper woods, shifts of two or three keeping me in sight, and when I stopped for rest and meals (times and rates outlined in the salvage contract) they waited for me, staring as if I were entertainment.

They are not at all feline in appearance. The closest analog I can think of is an otter, although *felis lutrina* has feathers rather than fur. The largest of them is about a meter long, and they move with a strange, buoyant grace, covering the land in long leaps. Their fifth leg is narrower and remains curled beneath them most of the time; it boasts very fine, sharp claws ideally suited to rooting insects out of the detritus of the forest floor.

Even if there are other mammals my size here, they would have seen nothing like my EnviroSuit. They should be afraid of me.

They should also have been made extinct 57 years ago.

Existence of specimens from the planet's original biome suggest faulty terraformer installation or maintenance, with unpredictable consequences for a standard salvage operation. The reassertion of indigenous plant life has forced me to land 165 kilometers away from the Main Terraformer Control Center and complete the exploratory journey on foot. Surcharges and overtime will be invoiced as outlined in the salvage contract.

HOURS BILLED: 15.75
COVERED BY PRE-PAY: 100%

THANK YOU FOR SELECTING
DEEP HAZARD SALVAGE SERVICE!
HAVE A NICE DAY!

[message not sent. error code 1104 atmospheric interference.]

DEFINITION: Amici Lagomorpha. *Indigenous pseudomammalian herbivore. Dependent on low-growing open fields for nutrients. Primary food source for indigenous carnivores. Does not hunt. Easily frightened but non-hostile.*

ADDENDUM: Virulently poisonous to humans unless consumed raw. Don't eat them. Really. They don't even taste good. At least that's what Tara said before the vomiting and brain death.

Day Two

Looks like at least one B42 Secondary Soil Module is still live.

This morning, after cutting through a particularly dense copse of thorn-bearing bushes, I stumbled into a clear-cut path 2.8 meters wide—the precise width of the B42's effective cutting capacity. Based on the growth of hecate moss, a cespitose perennial that should have been extinct along with *felis lutrinae*, the path is about seven terran weeks old. It seems likely the B42 was not properly maintained during its original run, and retained rootable debris from plants it was meant to eradicate.

The path has allowed me to make up some time. The were-kats seemed to prefer it as well, probably because both *amici lagomorphae* and a wide variety of slow, bulbous insects enjoyed grazing on the open growth. They spent most of the day dining.

Which is perhaps why later, after I'd made camp for the night, three of them approached me, one carrying a live *lagomorpha*. They dropped it at my feet and backed away, and the lagomorpha froze, staring up at me with very rabbit-like yellow eyes. The were-kats watched me in anticipation, but I did nothing until the *lagomorpha*'s paralysis broke and it bolted into the higher underbrush.

The were-kats sighed in disappointed unison and returned to their pack.

They are of course unaware I consume all nutrition via my EnviroSuit. But I did feel, in the moment, very much an inferior hunter.

Given the active B42, I must assume the terraformer shutdown transmitted 15 years ago was not successful, and manual shutdown will be required before salvage. Extra time for this operation will be billed at the overtime rate outlined in the salvage contract.

HOURS BILLED: 17.00
REBATE FOR RECLAIMED DISTANCE: 2.5
TOTAL HOURS BILLED: 30.25
COVERED BY PRE-PAY: 100%

THANK YOU FOR SELECTING
DEEP HAZARD SALVAGE SERVICE!
HAVE A NICE DAY!

[message not sent. error code 1104 atmospheric interference.]

DEFINITION: Titanium Viventum. *Molten product of stable eruptions, produced at regular intervals on the planet's surface. Thermal radiation tops 800 degrees Kelvin. Terraformer modules will fail within fifteen meters of the eruption zone. Steady effusion; no explosions recorded.*

ADDENDUM: People will fail within fifteen meters of the eruption zone, too (Ellsworth got greedy). But that's real titanium. No kidding. Shouldn't we be figuring out how to mine this stuff?

Day Three

It seems the original notes on the were-kats were incomplete.

After our lunchtime break, they didn't resume their usual scattered, loping progress, but clustered before me, all nine of them, their movements slow and hesitant, stopping frequently to sniff the air. After an hour of my EnviroSuit persistently showing no hazards ahead, I attempted to get around them, and for the first time since my arrival they turned on me, surrounding me while emitting a low-pitched rumble.

I had not really believed were-kats were capable of killing humans. But that sound...I know a threat when I hear one. I've seen a were-kat skin and part out a full-grown lagomorpha in less than five seconds. And they were closing in on me, none of the companionable friendliness of the last several days in evidence.

I wasn't worried about being eaten alive. Once they pierced my suit, the atmosphere would kill me in thirty seconds. It would have been merciful, at least, and I wouldn't have been the first—or last—salvage jockey to die for Deep Hazard. But I didn't want to die of poison gas, either. Or anything else.

I retreated as they closed, but it wasn't until I was forced off the path and into the woods that I recognized I was being herded.

Once I stopped resisting, their entire demeanor changed. No more threats, no more visions of having my suit ripped open and my eyes taken out by spiny needle teeth. Just me and my cheerful companions, hiking up and away from the safe path and into the dense woods where the footing was far more precarious. They bounded ahead of me, unencumbered by my size and my clothing, and I followed without question.

Eventually we broke into a clearing, and I was able to look down over where we'd come, all the way back to the B42 path where they'd threatened me.

Twenty meters ahead of where we'd veered off, concealed by tight, high thickets of thorny undergrowth, was a swamp that expanded into a red-and-white pit of hot lava.

I'd have been fine, of course. My thermal readout would have warned me, or I'd have noticed the change in the footing. I'd have paid attention and turned around like a sensible person, finding this alternative route all on my own.

But the were-kats didn't know that.

Addendum: It's the middle of the night, and I want to add this note before I forget.

I can't sleep well on solid rock, so it's no surprise I woke up when the were-kats approached my campsite. I stayed still as they nosed through my meager personal belongings until they came across my daily waste canister. Per regulations, I have been leaving them along our path to be collected on the way back to my ship.

It took two of them to lift it, winding their fifth legs around it like supple terran serpents. They carried it down the hill and into the woods, and returned—nearly half an hour later—empty-handed.

Damned if I don't think they dropped it in that lava pit.

The deviation from the path has added an extra 12 kilometers to my route. Additional time will be billed as outlined in the salvage contract.

```
HOURS BILLED: 19.00
TOTAL HOURS BILLED: 49.25
COVERED BY PRE-PAY: 18%
SURCHARGE: 3,331,2○
```

THANK YOU FOR SELECTING
DEEP HAZARD SALVAGE SERVICE!
HAVE A NICE DAY!

```
[message not sent. error code 1104 atmospheric
interference.]
```

DEFINITION: B42 Secondary Soil Module. *Removes native soil and replaces with terran-equivalent tillable material. Native soil sequenced and destroyed. Compatible components recycled as fertilizer.*

ADDENDUM: Also appears to save the DNA sequencing data locally, even after synching with the main controller, which means its memory fills up too quickly. We've had to retrieve and reset these things way more often than the manual says we should. Come on, people. Don't you test this stuff before you send it out?

Day Four

Found the rogue B42.

My first warning was when the were-kats disappeared, but I didn't think much of it. They hunt frequently during the day, usually in groups; it's only at night that I see all of them together, snoring, piled on each other like discarded socks.

But if my oxygen recycler hadn't had its hourly clean-and-reset cycle, leaving me with three full seconds of nothing but the unenhanced ambient noise of the woods around me, I wouldn't have heard the module coming, and I probably wouldn't have been able to outrun it.

As it was, I was frozen for nearly a full second before my training kicked in and I dashed away at an angle into the denser forest. The B42 almost caught my heel as it went by, methodically mulching undergrowth and scattering the pulverized result far into the woods.

I kept my hands over my head until my readout told me the B42 was out of range. When I stood up, the were-kats popped up around me, unconcerned with the disruption, then dropped to four legs and slunk along the ground until they reached the edge of the path cut by the B42. There they feasted for twenty full minutes, and then spent another twenty frolicking in the newly-exposed soil.

I fed a soil sample to my EnviroSuit's analyzer. Plenty of nitrogen and phosphorous, but the potassium was way off, and it hosted an entirely incongruous set of metals and trace elements. Not terran-compatible at all. The B42 was still live, but it wasn't converting a damn thing.

This could explain how the environment could be growing unchecked, but not how the original flora and fauna came to be resurrected. The terran environment was maintained here for 57 years; by now, 15 years post-shutdown, this place should have been barren dust, leftover oxygenated atmosphere clinging by a thread. It shouldn't have been habitable by anything—not even were-kats—for another six decades.

The were-kats, as has become their habit, brought me a selection of grubs and worms, feeding their hunting-impaired companion. They hold little nutritional value for humans, but they're not poisonous. Ground up, with a touch of umami, they taste like mushrooms.

```
HOURS BILLED: 14.5
TOTAL HOURS BILLED: 63.75
COVERED BY PRE-PAY: 0%
SURCHARGE: 7,112,1☿
```

```
             THANK YOU FOR SELECTING
          DEEP HAZARD SALVAGE SERVICE!
                 HAVE A NICE DAY!
```

```
[message not sent. error code 1104 atmospheric
interference.]
```

DEFINITION: Haven Systems Multi-Axis Full-Spectrum Terraformer, Model 8. *Overrides and eliminates existing environment, asserting and maintaining terran-compatible soil and atmosphere for the purpose of growing crops. Equipped with remote update capability, full safety shutdown protocols, and limited self-upgrading manufacturing abilities. Full warranty for 500 years or the heat death of the universe, whichever comes first.*

ADDENDUM: I'm quitting. I mean it. I don't care how hard it is for you to get more staff. Someone else can make the sacrifice to feed the galaxy. This thing was programmed by camphor addicts and spoiled children. Brings in more samples than it plants crops, and if we toss them? Just brings us more. This is the worst job I've ever had, and I've worked waist-deep in sewage in the asteroid caves. At least when you get rid of sewage it stays gone.

Day Five

It's still hard, sometimes, to realize all this has been replaced by single-module food fabrication units, cheap and simple to install.

I've salvaged larger terraformer complexes, but the Model 8 always presents the problem of the main housing. Later models modularized the biorecombinators and the atmospheric converters, but the Model 8 got some efficiency out of housing them both in a single large structure. Dismantling it involves removing the exterior walls entirely before piecing out the interior, and even with the large salvager it was going to take me weeks of work to clear the space.

The rest of the Model 8 was typical: crew quarters, Secondary Module housing, and control areas all built with standard polygonal prefab blocks. All in all, not a complicated salvage—except I still had to figure out how to turn it off.

Because it was still operating at full power. Everything. Even the recombinators. But in the previous four days, I didn't see a single terran plant, didn't pass through a single pocket of oxygenated atmosphere. Like the B42, it was running, but doing nothing.

Or maybe not nothing. Just not trying to turn this place into Earth.

The were-kats declined to enter the Control System cube with me, electing instead to mill around in the well-tamped dirt at the entrance. The space was strangely cozy, with small, square windows arranged in a single line half a meter from the ceiling, letting in the dim light of the planet's mid-morning. As soon as I sat down in front of the readout, the oxygenation system turned on, giving me air I could actually breathe. I pulled my helmet off for the first time in five days, and was hit by the odor of ozone and dust: nothing organic, not even a trace scent of old human sweat.

The auditory module synched with my EnviroSuit, and I tugged off my gloves and reached for the keyboard to scan through the system logs. It took some time to look back through five years' worth of entries to find the shutdown signal, but it was there, clean and clear:

```
22231405> INCOMING
22231406> SHUTDOWN[100,FULL,1] *// Immediate
shutdown requested
22231407> SHUTDOWN INITIATED *// Command sent
22231407> SHUTDOWN COMPLETED[2] *// Successful
shutdown Status 2
```

I've shutdown a lot of models of a lot of terraformers. Shutdown options are binary, always, for safety. Off or on. No ambiguity. Much smaller chance for error.

There is no 2 in binary.

"Why is the terraformer still operational?" I asked.

```
> SHUTDOWN SUCCESSFUL. COMPLETION STATUS 2.
```

"Define Status 2."

```
> FACTORY RESET.
```

I'm familiar with all the available upgrades on the Model 8, but it was possible I'd missed an option somewhere. Every terraformer has its quirks, after all, and even with close monitoring it's possible this one had been given a mod nobody'd logged.

Which didn't matter, really. The state of the terraformer—the state of the planet—didn't change my task. I'd been hired to take the thing away, modded or not. The only complication was figuring out how to shut it down properly without documentation.

"Show me the factory reset code."

```
(2)
IF SHUTDOWN
*// Fuck the system!!
ATMOSPHERICS[ORIGINAL] *// Put the damn
atmosphere back
BIODIVERSITY[REVERT] *// Reseed the fauna
ACCELERATE[2] *// Speed it the fuck up, dammit
X=WARNING[UNINHABITABLE,EVACUATE] *// Get the
humans off NOW
BROADCAST[X]
ENDIF
```

I don't tell people my mother was a revolutionary. Nobody wants to hire salvage with political opinions. She always told me we didn't have the right to terraform like this, to destroy an existing habitat to feed the billions of people we've scattered without compunction all over the galaxy.

I never really understood why she thought it was so bad to terraform a planet that didn't have any intelligent life on it. What's a few alien plants and animals? It's not like the universe is limited. It's not like there aren't more somewhere, even if we don't know where.

"How would terraformer shutdown affect the environment?"

> FULL ENVIRONMENTAL COLLAPSE WITHIN 15 TERRAN
YEARS.

"How much longer will the terraformer need to run to return the environment to self-sufficiency?"

> 17.4 TERRAN YEARS.

Like all Deep Hazard contracts, mine has a time limit: two terran years. Always more than enough. I've never had a salvage, no matter how complicated, take me more than six months. This one? Four to five weeks to dismantle, another two to transport the materials to my tug. An easy job. Easy money.

Were-kats have a short lifespan—five, six terran years if they manage to stay with a pack. My companions of the last few days would be long gone by the time the atmosphere failed.

If I left the terraformer, my reputation would be destroyed. I wouldn't get another salvage job again, ever. Not even critical hazmat.

I took a breath, getting ready to speak, and something outside exploded.

I ran to the window and peered into the distance, the were-kats in the yard frozen mid-frolic and staring with me. I saw the flare of a distant flame and braced myself for the roar of a fireball; but instead the light dimmed and died, and the were-kats returned to jumping and wrestling as if they'd never been disturbed.

When I turned back to the console, it was displaying a flashing line:

> ATTENTION! B42 SECONDARY SOIL MODULE 3 HAS MALFUNCTIONED. MANUAL RETRIEVAL REQUIRED.

And then:

> ?

The question mark didn't flash. It just sat there, waiting, and if I'd done nothing it would have waited until the end of the world.

[log erasure requested]
[logs erased]
[report re-initiated]

SALVAGE REPORT
Haven Systems Terraformer Model 8 (deactivated)

Day One

Arrival at the Letrus Terraformer Colony delayed due to engine maintenance issues.

Ship-to-shore sensors show high surface radiation, with the bulk of the terraformer structures destroyed and unsalvageable. I have identified a single intact B42 Secondary Soil Module, apparently trapped outside the Main Terraformer Control Center at shutdown time. It is outside the irradiated zone and should be salvageable in its entirety.

Due to the diminished amount of material obtained on this effort, I have reduced my usual fee and credited the overpaid amount. Delivery time of the B42 Secondary Soil Module should be 7 to 10 days.

HOURS BILLED: 10.5
COVERED BY PRE-PAY: 100%
REFUND: 6,231,7☿

THANK YOU FOR SELECTING

DEEP HAZARD SALVAGE SERVICE!
HAVE A NICE DAY!

[message sent.]

THE HAUNTING OF JESSICA LOCKWOOD

A CENTRAL CORPS SHORT

I.

"You know, Jess," Tierney called out from the rushes, a good twenty meters from the shoreline, "it could have been a lot worse."

Jessica stood waist-deep in the salt-saturated water, curling her toes into the silt. The heat was interminable, here in the late summer; but they'd been greeted lately by unusually dry days, the humidity hovering around 80%, the breezes off the Rian Sea reaching as far inland as the habitat buildings set deep in the jungle. Gone were the acrid odors of decaying riddlebugs and spongifruit ruptured in the heat; instead she could smell the must of the rushes and the flowering needle grass, and the only sounds the wind carried were the knocking of the pneumo-tree leaves and the sleepy hum of sand crickets preparing to lay eggs for overwinter.

The bright sun was invigorating, the water felt cool on Jessica's skin, and Tierney was absolutely wrong: it couldn't possibly have been worse.

Aunt Pella had told her the night before the council would

push for a severe sentence. "They'll take into account your age," Pella had said, "but they can't ignore the seriousness of the crime. Jessica—" Here Pella had stopped, staring down at Jessica with her usual severe expression— "whatever they say, whatever choices they give you, take your night to decide. It's your legal right."

Jessica had figured that meant her decision would be an easy one. Jessica had also figured Pella would be at her side at the sentencing to advise her, but Pella hadn't appeared in the courtroom that morning. Instead Jessica had been left alone, standing before Alder James, fully half the town seated in the gallery behind her, as she was sentenced to work in the infirmary until she turned nineteen.

Five standard years. Nearly forty seasons. Learning *medicine*. And monitored every minute of her day, no software shadows or memory strips or anything she was any good at, anything that was any fun. Like she was *dangerous*. All these people she'd known her whole life, treating her like a criminal.

Which she was, of course. There was no avoiding that much.

She sank into the water and came up again, the cool streaming through her hair and down her back. "At least they let me go to the beach," she called back to Tierney, forcing some cheer into her voice. Tierney was only trying to help, after all. None of this was Tierney's fault. None of this was anyone's fault but Jessica's, and she was going to pay for it with the next five years of her life. Because Alder James' alternative sentence had been nothing but a joke.

"Optionally, you may choose to be banished from Tengri for fifteen standard years, to leave the planet before the next Umé Rise."

She'd expected some nominal support from the gallery—a cry, or at least one or two outraged gasps—but there had been only silence. And she had almost broken her long-standing rule against crying in public.

The council had followed the law, giving her two appropriate punishments to choose from. Except one of them would strip every joy from her life, and the other would throw her out, alone and helpless, into a strange and hostile galaxy she knew nothing of at all.

"Come on in," she called to Tierney, but didn't wait when her friend shook their head. Tierney hated the beach, never mind it was the only place within easy travel distance that offered relief from the dense, sticky jungle. Jessica suspected Tierney had a phobia of water; Tierney accompanying her at all was a kindness born of their long friendship. Jessica resolved, as she often did, to be a better friend, and maybe earn some of Tierney's goodness for once.

She dove, and kicked her way down to the ocean floor. *This might be all right. Sea and sand, Tierney waiting for me on the shore, even if the security people are following me everywhere and everyone thinks I'm some vile criminal and I'll never touch a logic core again.*

She surfaced to find Aunt Pella treading water next to her, the salty water dripping off her dark curls.

Jessica's hard-won spark of optimism died in a wave of hurt. *Where were you?* she wanted to shout, but her throat was too tight. She supposed Pella had joined her here in a show of support; Pella disliked swimming almost as much as Tierney did. But Jessica had needed Pella that morning, in court, when she'd felt small and vulnerable and terrified she'd screwed up her life with a prank.

"It wasn't, though, was it?" said Pella, as if she'd been following Jessica's thoughts. Her eyes, vivid blue against skin nearly as pale as Jessica's, held deep disappointment.

You can't be disappointed with me, Jessica thought. *Right now I'm disappointed with you.* "I didn't hurt anybody," she tried.

"Hmph." Pella swam closer, turning her sharp-featured face to the afternoon sunshine. "You took what belonged to all of us, to the whole colony, and you gave it away. What was the purpose of that?"

Jessica hadn't, initially, thought about giving the money away at all. It was supposed to be like all her previous pranks, apart from the scope: moving money into the wrong accounts, misplacing deposit records, creating tangles of mistaken commits and dead-end memory shadows that would take the colony techs weeks to unravel. A victimless crime; Tengri almost never needed actual currency. Their trade was research, and it was only their relative isolation in the Second Sector that subjected them to the occasional thin season. She never pulled anything when starvation loomed, and she'd never moved the money somewhere unrecoverable.

But this time...the summer flu had been so bad. Every eightday had brought a funeral for at least three people. Her cohort had been untouched this time—the first time in years—and that had left her feeling both grateful and guilty. Tierney's cohort had lost four: three adults and a child, the newest infant, infected despite their rigorous attempts to isolate her.

And every funeral was followed by a feast on the town common, where the dead were praised for their contribution to the colony's research, Tengri's one-and-only export. Every death produced value, medical research that saved lives all across the galaxy. It shouldn't have made Jessica angry. It didn't seem to make anyone else angry. But when she'd triggered the code to funnel the colony's fall seawall maintenance budget into an anonymous off-world PSI food charity, she'd said *research THIS* out loud.

"I don't know why I did it," she told Pella, aware she sounded sulky.

Pella scoffed, a very un-Pella-like sound. "You do," she insisted. "You just think I'll be angry with you for it."

"I don't *know*," Jessica repeated. "We didn't need the money, not this year. Other people might." She met Pella's eyes. "Maybe there's more we can do for the galaxy than just let our people die."

"You think it's either-or? Cash or research?" Pella's expression finally softened, and she kicked herself closer, resting a hand on

Jessica's shoulder. Her fingers were needle-grass thin, her touch rough with drying salt. "Every day is a choice, you know," she said. "A choice to steal from the colony. A choice to tell the truth when you were on trial, even though you could have lied. And now you choose how you'll atone." Her hand dropped back into the water. "You already know what you want, Jessica. It's just that you don't yet see."

"Jessica!" Tierney was calling from the shore, and Jessica turned to find she'd drifted out further than she'd thought.

"I have to go," she said, looking back over her shoulder; but Pella had vanished. No splash, no farewell, not even a ripple. She was gone as if she'd never been there.

Jessica blinked at the glare off the water. Was she really that tired? Had she manufactured that entire conversation in her head? Puzzled, she turned back to the waterfront, and saw her security detail standing with Tierney, all three of them waving her furiously back to shore.

2.

Alder James' voice was strained. "You said she wasn't seriously ill."

"This morning she wasn't," said Alder Hazel, in her usual academic tone. "Now she is."

Jessica sat in one of the wide, comfortable armchairs they provided for relatives in the infirmary, and watched Pella sleep. Pella had been tranquilized after her fever had driven her to delirium, half an hour before they'd contacted Jessica's guards.

Pella had been unconscious before Jessica had gone in swimming. Drugged when Jessica had spoken to...*someone* in the shallows of the Rian Sea.

James and Hazel continued arguing behind her, their voices low and strained. Part of Jessica wondered if Alder James had ever, even when he was young, expressed concern with anything other than anger. The rest of her studied Pella with her short life-time's worth of clinical skill, fighting panic, searching for signs of hope. Pella's breathing was steady, but her color was concerning: her skin, light pink thanks to Tengri's endless sunny days, had an odd yellow-green cast, as if her blood wasn't quite making it to the surface.

Jessica had lost siblings throughout the years. The last time she'd lost a parent, she'd been too young to remember.

Pella had to survive this. There was no other option.

"Jessica."

She looked up, abruptly aware James had been saying her name for a while. He stood over her with his usual stiff formality, his expression back to its usual mask, but she thought, now that she was looking for it, the skin underneath his eyes looked vaguely bruised.

Something in those eyes relaxed a little, and it crossed her mind he might be feeling sorry for her. "If you'd like," he said, his voice as close to gentle as she'd ever known it, "you can stay here. Just tell your security detail if you need to leave the room."

So this is what her sentence would be like, even when one of her parents was dying.

Now you choose how you'll atone.

"Thank you, Alder James," she said, and surprised herself by meaning it.

He left shortly afterward, and Jessica curled up in the chair next to Pella's bed, lost in a swirl of worry until the day's events tugged her down into sleep.

"Come on, Jessie," whispered a voice in her ear. "We don't have a lot of time."

Jessica woke, blinking in the darkness of the dimly lit ward. Tierney stood next to her, only it wasn't her Tierney. It was

Tierney at six, cherubic and sparkly-eyed, expression perpetually cheerful. A dream, then, and Jessica felt a wave of relief; nothing that happened in a dream could hurt Pella, or her, or anybody else.

Small!Tierney's round fingers closed over Jessica's wrist and tugged. "It won't take long."

Jessica looked over at Pella. Her chest rose and fell with reassuring steadiness. *In my dream, at least, she's stable.* Reluctantly, she got to her feet, and let Small!Tierney grasp her hand.

The child pulled Jessica out of the infirmary and down through the wide forest road to the habitat clearing. Only it wasn't the clearing Jessica knew: there were houses missing. Alder Neryssa's big multi-storey complex, put together for her never-ending supply of children, was instead a grove of sickly overshadowed pneumo-trees; Alder Cait's open cottage—no walls, no bedrooms, only the baths shielded from general view—was absent, the spot it would be built on covered in low-growing lavender root. Invasive stuff, Jessica recalled; it had taken Cait's cohort three years of aggressive weeding to kill it off.

The past, then. Six years ago at least.

Small!Tierney steered them unerringly toward Jessica's house, one of the oldest structures in the habitat. Two storeys only, all the rooms small; but the roof line was all uneven angles and curves, providing the children the best hide-and-seek in the colony. Small!Tierney climbed the leatherroot vine on the outside of the house, and Jessica clambered up after them, trying not to remember she was far too big to be doing this now.

Small!Tierney let them in through the upper landing window, turned long enough to hold a finger up to their lips, then crept out into the hall. Jessica followed.

Sitting on the landing, her feet threaded through the balusters, was another child. Light skin, small nose, thick eyebrows edging toward each other as she frowned; hair, curly and red, escaping in wild tendrils from two haphazard pigtails. Taller than

Tierney, still; the last season that would be true. Her feet swung, just a little; she was silent, her eyes on the light from the room below.

"It's all right," Small!Tierney said. "She can't see you."

Jessica crept forward, then lowered herself down next to her childhood self.

Voices came up from below: adults arguing. She recognized Pella's voice right away, and then the other, deep and stern: Alder James.

Her stomach rolled over. She knew what night this was.

"No," she said, and moved to get up.

Small!Tierney patted her shoulder, and in the way of dreams, Jessica's limbs were abruptly weighted with lead. "It's okay. It won't be what you think."

Of course it would be.

"You can't do this to her," Pella was saying. She sounded angry, passionate; Jessica hadn't remembered Pella being so out of control. "Do you know how much she's lost?"

"We all know how much she's lost." Alder James' voice was infuriatingly calm. "That's not the point, Pella. We only have room for one more this year, and we've already acquired enough from her genetic line."

"'Genetic line.'" Pella spat the words out. "What about her *heart*, James? We're all so good at telling everyone their loss is for the good of all, but when it comes time for us to take care of each other, we're all about chemicals and DNA." Jessica heard the clink of glasses; Pella was pouring drinks. "You've known Clara all her life, just like I have. She needs a baby. Even with all the ones she's lost, she's always been at the front of the volunteer line. And she cares for all of her children, even the ones she didn't birth. You can't say that about everyone around here."

"Indeed." Alder James sounded vaguely amused, and Jessica wondered if Pella was glaring at him. "I'm not trying to hurt Clara," he said, and his voice had softened, just a little. "But we can't alter reality. We had a bad harvest last fall. It's going to be a near thing with the children we've already allocated. My other choice was no new babies at all, but with the summer flu so bad..." He trailed off, and there was silence for a moment. "I'll tell her myself," he said at last. "In the morning."

"No." Pella's voice was calm now, but Jessica couldn't remember ever hearing her so weary. "I'll do it. Let her be angry with me. Let her think I used my influence to take her place. But next year, James, I want her first in line."

"I can't promise that."

"But you'll try."

There was another long silence. Jessica looked down at Small!Jessica; her lower lip had extended. She'd never been much for tears when she was younger, she recalled; most of her sorrow had taken the shape of anger. *Like Alder James.* She wondered when that had stopped.

"Thank you for the drink, Pella," he said, and then Jessica heard footsteps. The pair appeared in the entryway below them; Pella's hair was longer, her corkscrew curls pulled into a long dark plait down her back, but even eight years younger James was already gray. To Jessica's surprise, he bent down as they reached the door, and Pella kissed him, not entirely begrudgingly.

Well that's *news.*

The door closed behind Alder James, and Pella stood with her palm against it. And then she said, "You can come down now."

Beside her, Small!Jessica kept frowning; but she pulled her legs back through the balusters and got to her feet. Jessica followed suit, glancing at Small!Tierney, who was watching the entire scene with delight. Tierney's family had had two new children that year, Jessica recalled; both had lived through the winter, but only because PSI had shown up with a supply of fresh produce they needed to unload before it spoiled. Or that's what they'd been told; Central's colonies weren't supposed to appeal directly to PSI for help, but it wasn't like people on Tengri didn't have plenty of ways to send an untraceable message. Jessica had honed her hacking skills with the best in the sector.

Jessica trailed Small!Jessica, who was in no hurry. Pella was watching the little girl with a patient smile on her face. Jessica hadn't remembered how different Pella had been back then: still tall and straight, but rounder, softer, more relaxed, less guarded. Small!Jessica took each stair in two steps as if steadying herself, although Jessica remembered being perfectly agile at the age of six. When Small!Jessica made it down the stairs, Pella crouched in front of her. "Are you all right, little one?"

Small!Jessica kept scowling. "Scottie's dead."

That had been his name: Scott Aloysius Haigh, and hadn't they all laughed at such a big name for a small baby. The summer flu had run late that year, and he'd caught it at the end, when they'd all thought it was done, when nobody worried anymore about quarantining the small ones or keeping them inside.

Pella's face grew sad, and she reached out, tucking a coiled lock behind Small!Jessica's ear. "I know, honey. I'm sorry. I know you loved him."

"We all loved him."

Watching, Jessica felt a wave of rage. They'd been taught that phrase from birth, all of them, like a mantra: death was a shared experience. Grief was never exclusive, and it was never private. It was true, always true, but the phrase had always left Jessica wanting to dive to the bottom of the sea and scream until she ran out of air.

Pella's hand strayed to Small!Jessica's cheek. "We did," she agreed. "But...it's okay to be sad, honey."

The child's scowl didn't shift. "I'm not sad."

Pella's lips quirked again. "It's okay to be angry, too, you know."

And at that, Small!Jessica's lower lip started to tremble, and she burst into tears, and Pella wrapped her arms around the child and held her close.

What Jessica had not seen all those years ago, when Pella let her grieve a baby she had barely known, was Pella's own eyes squeezing shut, her silent tears falling into Small!Jessica's unruly hair.

3.

Jessica woke to Alder James' voice behind her. "She's looking better," he said.

Jessica stayed still, feigning sleep. James still sounded worried.

"We'll see how she fares in the morning," said Hazel.

Jessica considered opening her eyes, seeking company, comfort. Instead she curled tighter into the chair and kept her eyes closed.

The night was cooler, but the humidity was picking up, and Jessica's skin prickled indecisively. This had to be what was bringing on the dreams; she never slept soundly when the weather turned odd. She'd heard of colony worlds that were cooler, which didn't appeal at all; but she thought, sometimes, she might like someplace a little drier. Earth, they said, was drier, at least away from the vast oceans. She'd never studied it. She'd never thought about going anywhere else at all.

She was standing in the main town road. Next to her stood Alder!James, dressed in the same somber, formal suit he'd worn at her sentencing, fingers flexing with impatience. Before them was the flat-roofed council center, and she wondered who would possibly choose that staid, dull building at this hour.

"It's common for us to gather here at night," Alder!James told her. "It's cool, and it's easy to talk. Come and sit. And be still; you must listen as well as watch."

They passed through the wide main door, and the night's

humidity vanished, dissipated by the building's dehumidifiers. There were still chairs set up from the last town meeting, row after row, straight as if they'd never been used. Near the center dais, there were three people clustered around one of the big cooling units. One was Alder James—the real one, it seemed, whatever that meant in this dream—leaning back in an armchair, legs crossed, still and silent. Alder Sarah sat next to him, elbows on her knees, hands balled into fists. Before both of them paced Alder Ceredig, tall, spidery-thin, and uncharacteristically animated. As they drew closer, Jessica could hear Ceredig's voice, sharp and angry.

"That was utter foolishness," Ceredig said, and even before she and Alder!James sat in the chairs opposite the trio, she could see Sarah's knuckles go white.

"It's the law," Sarah told him. "She's still a child. She gets a choice."

Jessica decided she liked dreams better when they were not about her.

Ceredig stopped pacing and turned on Sarah, his glare so fierce Jessica found herself drawing back. "Yes, Sarah. She's still a child. We're not finished raising her. And what have we just told her? We've told her we don't want her anymore."

"Don't be absurd. Nobody wants her to leave."

"Then what was the point of telling her she could?"

Alder James broke into their argument. "It's the choice that's the point," he said, but his tone was distracted, as if his mind wasn't really on the conversation. "She's smart, Ceredig. Smart and healthy, and bored out of her mind. She needs adult responsibilities, so we gave her one. We let her choose her fate."

Ceredig turned his ire on James. "And what if she'd told us she was leaving?" Ceredig asked. "You'd just let her go?"

"That's never going to happen," Sarah snapped.

"You'd better hope it doesn't," Ceredig declared. "Do you

know how few in her cohort have been as resistant as she is to disease? We need—"

And that, it seemed, was enough for James. "We need," he clarified, "better quarantine protocols. This strain wasn't even that virulent, and we still lost twenty-seven children. Or have you forgotten?"

Jessica drew a breath between her teeth as Ceredig's expression froze, his complexion washing with ash. Ceredig's cohort had lost an entire generation, all their children between nine and seventeen, before the flu had even reached full strength.

Ceredig swallowed and turned away from the others, and Jessica could see his face shift from anger to haunted grief. His hands began to clench like Sarah's. "Tell me, James," he said, his voice calmer, "has there ever been anyone in your life you haven't manipulated?"

James should have looked insulted; instead, a look Jessica couldn't identify flashed briefly across his face before his expression closed again. "I don't manipulate, Ceredig." He got to his feet and took a step toward the older man. "We protect who we can here. Jessica doesn't need our protection anymore."

Ceredig swallowed, and Jessica saw his eyes brighten.

Behind the two men, Sarah threw up her hands. "You're both hopeless," she said, getting to her feet with them. "Of course we need her. And of course she needs our protection. You're both wrong, and I hope you're happy." She strode past Jessica and Alder!James, and her footsteps faded behind them.

James and Ceredig stood silent for a moment. Ceredig blinked and straightened, and when he finally spoke, his voice didn't tremble at all. "Sarah's got it backward, you know," he told James.

Alder James nodded. "It doesn't matter. She's chosen."

"I hope you're wrong."

And Alder James did something Jessica had almost never seen —he laughed, although Jessica didn't think he'd found anything

Ceredig said amusing. "I hope I'm wrong, too, Ceredig. I'm selfish enough for that."

Ceredig coughed out a laugh as well, and Jessica was left wondering what the hell they were talking about.

4.

Jessica stirred at the sound of a sheet being pulled back. She opened her eyes to find Alder Hazel standing over Pella, gently and methodically changing the bedsheet out from under her.

"Do you need help?" Jessica asked.

"No, thank you, dear," said Alder Hazel.

Jessica's stomach tightened. Hazel never called anyone *dear*.

She drew the back of her hand across her eyes. Hazel wasn't one to invite confidence, but there was no one else to talk to. "I don't want her to die, Alder Hazel."

Hazel sighed. "There's always hope, Jessica. Until there isn't."

She turned and left, and Jessica curled up again, watching Pella's chest rise and fall, rise and fall.

The room was illuminated by bright white moonlight, and Pella's bed was empty.

Jessica blinked once, and unfolded her legs out from under her. She knew the feel of it now, the odd hyper-reality directed by something outside of herself, and she got to her feet, looking around for her escort. She'd never seen the moonlight so bright, at least not that she could remember; perhaps it was the hour, or perhaps—she turned to the window, and Pella was standing there, her back to Jessica, her dark hair haloed by the light. Beyond her was the treeline, and in the sky hung Tengri's three moons in a row: Umé, Cleite, and Erlik, smallest to largest, although Jessica remembered, vaguely, that Erlik was nearly as small as Umé, just much closer.

A tri-moon. There were no tri-moons due for twenty years.

Pella's hair floated around her head as a breeze skittered its way through the room, tickling Jessica's skin, carrying the strong odors of compost and needle grass. Spring, then, before the summer heat wave, before the most deadly of the flus were due to arrive. Tierney always said spring breezes made them feel hopeful. The breezes always filled Jessica with dread.

She got up from the chair and moved next to Pella. The breeze had stilled, but Pella's hair kept floating. Jessica glanced at her profile. The monochrome lighting cast her skin silver-gray, but her expression was calm, contemplative, as if Jessica had caught her mid-idea. Without meeting Jessica's eyes, Pella turned and began walking toward the back of the hospital, her feet not making a sound.

Jessica followed her.

The rest of the hospital was empty, each bed made up neatly, none of the monitoring systems activated. The calm before the storm. Jessica shivered, and had to run to catch Pella, who was ignoring the empty ward and heading for the hallway to the research center.

The future research center was nearly unrecognizable. The square banks of shadow-and-stripe memory were gone, replaced by a set of domes clustered in the corners of the room, humming with a tone nearly too low for Jessica to hear. Much of the room was empty space, although Jessica knew in a few weeks it would be full of researchers poring over genome and chemical data on whatever the latest summer strain was. They'd parse and experiment and study each patient who came in, whether they lived or died; the data would be aggregated into conclusions about prevention and treatment and inoculation and shipped out to Central Gov for distribution to all Six Sectors. They saved lives, every year, all over the galaxy. Sometimes millions. Tengri Colony existed to find ways to save people. They did it by watching their own die.

There was a solitary figure seated at the far end of the research table, huddled over a dim display, one finger pushing at the rows of numbers. Pella stopped at the head of the table, her expression still thoughtful, her hair still floating; Jessica moved around her to approach the researcher. Slightly built, her arms and legs thin more from lack of food than nature; skin pale, although how pale was difficult to tell in the shadows. Her hair was smoothed back into a severe knot at the nape of her neck, and Jessica didn't have to note the color or the few escaping corkscrew tendrils to know who she was looking at.

Adult!Jessica was frowning at the numbers before her, scrolling back and forth as if she was looking for something. Next to the display, Adult!Jessica's left hand made quick notes now and then, but she'd written very little. Jessica drew closer, squinting at the information, but the numbers meant nothing to her. This was not a logic core or a memory shadow; this was something far more mundane. This was research, and from the expression on Adult!Jessica's face, she wasn't finding what she was looking for.

"It's late."

Jessica looked up, startled, and saw a figure standing next to Pella: thin, like his younger self, but more worn; gaunt and wizened, gray hair streaked with bright white. Alder James, recognizable if emaciated; they must have had some lean years for him to look so wiry and fragile.

Perhaps it wasn't only the years.

"I can't sleep," Adult!Jessica said, her eyes never leaving the numbers.

"You'll make mistakes." Alder!James made his way around the table.

Jessica bit down on annoyance; everything he said was always so discouraging. But Adult!Jessica didn't seem bothered. "All the worst mistakes are behind us," she said, and Jessica heard, then, how hoarse she sounded, how strained.

She waited for James' annoyed sigh, his admonishment of her negativity, his direction to focus on her task. None of it came. "We couldn't have predicted," he said, and his voice was gentle, almost hesitant.

"Of course we could." Adult!Jessica's tone was abruptly aggressive. Apparently, in her dreams at least, Jessica had figured out how to stand up to Alder James. "It's the same every year. It's just the severity and the timing." She flipped through the numbers. "There are answers here. There always have been. We just need to find them."

James moved to stand next to Adult!Jessica; and then, to Jessica's shock, he sat down next to her, leaning forward, hands open in appeal. "We do," he agreed, his voice still quiet. "But we don't have to find them tonight."

"Then when, James?" Adult!Jessica's voice had grown louder, and Jessica heard in its undertones a deep well of anguish. "Everything we learn, everything we find—we can't protect them. Year after year we can't, and I don't know why—"

Adult!Jessica's voice broke, and James put a hand over her arm, pulling her away from her data. "I'm sorry, Jessica," he said, and Jessica had never heard him sound so helpless before.

Adult!Jessica shook her head, silent for a moment as she swallowed tears. "It's our duty, isn't it?" she said. There was bitterness in her voice, bitterness Jessica knew well; but there was also weariness, resignation, *defeat*.

When had she become defeated?

"You're not alone, you know," James told her. "We're with you, all of us. We all know your grief."

Adult!Jessica sighed, and she shuddered, head to toe, as if the emotion was draining out through her feet. "I know," she said, and her voice was calmer. "I don't mean to be selfish. Please don't think—"

He squeezed her arm. "That's not what I meant, Jessie." How unsettling, that nickname coming from the man Jessica had only ever seen as an authority. "I meant—you don't have to be the one to do this. We can all do it. And we can all do it tomorrow, when we're rested, and the dead have had time to spread throughout the sea."

Adult!Jessica stilled. Something in Alder James's words, something in his kindness, had hit her wrong, had brought back whatever had driven her to be alone in this space in the middle of the night. "Those dead," she said quietly, "are mine, James. No matter how much you all loved them, they're my cohort. And I know what you'll say. I know I'll find others. I always find others." Her laugh was dry, and lost, and empty. *Empty*. Her life here had left her empty. "But tonight, my friend, they are gone on the currents. And I'd rather be alone here, doing something useful, than alone at home."

She started scrolling through the numbers again.

Alder!James watched her for several minutes, his hand still on her arm. Adult!Jessica didn't look at him, but surely she could see him out of the corner of her eye: rigid, helpless, wanting so much to say or do something that might help her.

After a moment he dropped his hand.

Jessica thought he would stand, would leave Adult!Jessica alone. Instead he turned to the table, tapped something behind his ear, and a data set appeared before his eyes. He began to scroll through the information, taking notes, and they worked together in silence in the still, warm room.

Jessica looked away from them. Not just a bad harvest year. A bad year for everything.

Pella had gone to a window, and she was again a silent, backlit figure.

"I don't know what this means," Jessica said. Her calm had entirely left her.

Pella didn't move.

"We lose people all the time," Jessica said. "Is that the lesson? That I shouldn't love so much?" *Fuck* that. "You're telling me I'm going to lose everything, so I have to find meaning in it? That this colony is more than just me and my petty discontents?" She was shaking; she wondered if the dream would let her pick up a chair, throw it across the room. "Why did you show me this? Why this moment? Everybody loses people here all the time, Tengri isn't just me, and I *know* that, but I don't know what you want me to do about it! I don't—"

Pella shifted, one arm jerking, as if she were pulling against a tether. Her figure hunched, shuddered, glitched; the moonlight made her solid then transparent, black to silver to white so bright Jessica couldn't look at her. Jessica blinked and held a hand over her eyes, shading away the worst of the tri-moon glare; Pella turned, jerky and clumsy, as if the effort were pulling her apart, and Jessica saw her face.

Her face.

Her skin was no longer smooth, no longer silvered; it wrinkled and tore and gaped away from her skull, the heat decay of days, a body left alone and not found in time for a proper cremation. But she wasn't dead: her eyes, pale and wide and terrified, searched Jessica's face, all desperation and urgency, and one arm, thin and skeletal, hand only half-covered in corrupt flesh, reached out.

Pella mouthed the word three times before Jessica understood it: *Run.*

Jessica ran.

5.

She startled awake to the sunrise streaming through the infirmary windows. Before her in the bed lay Pella, and her blue eyes were wide open, and they saw nothing at all.

6.

Nearly the entire colony attended Pella's funeral.

It was set at the equinox, after the summer flu season was officially over. Pella was the last casualty, as Scottie had been so long ago. The line to honor her stretched from the central government building through the habitat square down through the tall, knocking pneumo-trees and to the shore. There Alder James made a speech, and those who attended swore that his voice, always so controlled, held actual warmth and emotion. There were tears throughout, and when Pella's ashes were scattered into the salty sea, her cohort stood in a circle and sang an old hymn that Pella had loved.

Jessica was already off-world.

The day Pella died she felt drained and shattered and more certain of herself than she had ever been in her life. She might have taken it as a slight when she found Alder James had already contacted the freighter *Agincourt* and asked them to swing by that afternoon to pick up a passenger. She might have felt shoved away, second-guessed, mistrusted. Instead she'd thrown her arms around him, and the strange, taciturn man had actually managed to return the embrace, if only for a moment or two.

"Do great things," he said to her, and in her heart, amidst the fear and grief and loss, a spark of hope she'd thought long lost caught and flared and started to burn.

OVERLAY

WRITTEN BY ELIZABETH BONESTEEL FOR THE VERGE

... 4 *0%... 50%... 75%... 98%... Upload complete. Initiating connection.*

"—there, Ray? Do you read?"

"Affirmative. I read you, Cass."

Ray blinked into the dim light, waiting for the schematic overlay to come into focus.

Reception was good, even here in the fragrant, unwashed drains under the government lab, but uploads threw him every time. Vertigo. Nausea. Sometimes memory gaps. There were meds that could help him deal with it, but they all made him sleepy.

The mission didn't accommodate sleepy.

The cool damp was seeping under his skin, and the odor of raw sewage wasn't doing his stomach any good. Apparently, not even in their own buildings did the government pay for pre-treating waste. Closing his eyes to block out the mottled fiber-glass walls, Ray centered the overlay on the neon blue *R* that traced his movements within the green lines of the sewer drains. Cass' vivid *C* was on the other end of the building, moving cautiously north as she performed her own recon.

Above them both, in the red-outlined schematic of the locked-down federal building, he saw three amorphous red-orange spots indicating heat. No way to know through the building's leaded floor which one was Ando, but all three were motionless.

Damn.

"We've taught him to keep still since he was a baby," Cass said in his ear. "Don't read into it."

She was talking to herself as much as him, Ray knew. At 15, Ando was already a skilled operative, both level-headed and technically adept. But he'd gone off on his own for this one, and Cass was suffering from a debilitating case of delayed helicopter parenting. Ray had spent their journey here reassuring her that Ando knew how to take care of himself, never confessing the roiling terror in his own stomach. There was nothing quite like parenting to remind you how little of the universe you could control.

"I'm not reading anything into it," he lied. "I'm trying to figure out which one is him. This the best data you could get?"

"Government labs don't label their floor plans. But based on the power grid, the middle one is the computer lab. Too much drone traffic for him to hide there." Cass took a breath in his ear. "Flip a coin, Ray. We only get one chance at this."

Ray focused on his own blue icon and let his peripheral vision filter out distractions. There it was: a variance, almost insignificant, probably just the overlay's augmentors working to enhance the little they could make out through the interference. "The north spot," he said to Cass. "Full boost."

Ray felt a twinge in his left eye as the overlay flickered. The orange spot in the northern corner of the building grew larger and more pixelated, turning red, then yellow, then white, filling his field of vision. Too large to be an animal, too hot to be a drone.

Was it moving? He was sure it was moving. Ando was there. He had to be.

The twinge flared into a stabbing pain, and the room became another place: silhouettes; unintelligible whispers; a familiar odor, metallic and musty, out of place The brightness burned through his senses until there was nothing else left. No shadows, no sound, nothing but searing white emptiness and voices—

———

"—calibrate a little better. See that line there? We just—"
Upload suspended. Buffering... resuming... Upload complete.
"Dad?"

———

"Who's there?"

Ray stood in the open doorway of the building's north library. The voice had been low, worried—Ando's, yet not. His own, perhaps? Why would he be calling for his father? His father had been dead for 12 years.

How had he entered the building? Through the sewer?

That wavering call again. "Dad?"

It was Ando after all.

The boy came out of the shadows and threw his arms around his father, fear and relief tempering his usual teenaged reticence. "I've got him, Cass," Ray said, relief washing over him in a dizzying wave. For a moment, he wasn't an operative on a rescue mission, but a father with his only child in his arms, safe and unhurt.

Cass, never one for sentiment, handled the situation in her usual fashion. "You tell him I'm taking his fabricator and his cryptography equipment, and he can *handwrite* notes to his friends for the next 30 years," she ranted. "And he can leave the anarchy to the grown-ups."

Ray felt Ando choke out a laugh despite the danger. The boy knew his mother.

"Surveillance?" Ray asked.

"One drone sweep every 21 minutes," Ando said into his chest. "Two minutes until it's back."

"Back down into the sewers," Cass directed. "We can get out the south door."

Ando said, "We can't leave."

Ray loosed his arms, and Ando took a step away from him, his eyes level with his father's. Ray frowned, uneasy. When had Ando become so tall?

The boy's jaw was set, but there was no anger in his face; this was determination, not rebellion. "I came here to do this," Ando said. "I can't leave until it's done."

"You can do it another day!" Cass howled.

But Ray knew what the boy was thinking. "They'll be ready for us another day," he said. "He's right, Cass. We need to finish it."

She swore, repeatedly, a sailor's grand lexicon of profanity. "Fine," she said when her vocabulary was exhausted. "But you've got 85 seconds to get out of the way of that drone."

The overlay flickered, and abruptly, Ray could see in Ando's face the man he would one day become: a solid jaw, cheeks still cherubic when he smiled, wisdom drawing deep lines around those passionate eyes, wires of silver threaded through his jet-black hair. Ray shook himself. The boy was barely shaving, and Ray was seeing visions of him as an old man.

He gave Ando a quick nod, and with nothing but the flash of a grin, the boy disappeared into the shadows again. Now, of course, Ray had to remember how he'd reached the library. Surely, he'd come up through a floor panel or an auxiliary stairwell, but his memory provided nothing. "Cass?" he asked. "Where is it? The sewer entrance?"

The overlay flashed white.

———

"—on, just give it a se—"

———

He was in the building's main hallway. Behind him, he heard a low hum, possibly his imagination or maybe the patrol drone making its preprogrammed way down the hall, about to turn the corner to detect him. Everything they'd done, all of Ando's naive determination, would be for naught. He turned and ran from the sound, but there were no stairwells, no open doors, not even the room where he'd found Ando, and why was everything growing brighter? A corner up ahead. Surely, that's where he'd come in, that's where he'd left Ando, that's where—

———

"—interrupts expected at this stage. They've been working on the problem for a while. In the next—"

Buffering... 30%... 65%... 98%... Connection resumed.

———

What problem? What connection? Where am I?

Now, he was standing in a room lit by a bank of computer monitors. Before him sat Ando, tapping at an old-style physical keyboard, entirely absorbed in his task. Cass stood next to their son, staring anxiously up at Ray. His perception of his wife was apparently time-traveling as well: she looked to him as young and elegant as she had the first time she'd shown up at one of his protest meetings.

They'd made it to the computer room. Of course they had.

"I'm okay," he assured her. "Where are we?"

"We're overloading the main generator," Cass told him. "The auxiliaries should go up in sequence."

Well, that seemed sloppy. "No redundancies?"

"Tons of redundancies." She grinned at him, and there was pain in his left eye again along with a bright white flash, like an ancient camera. "Just no fail-safes."

---

just no fail-safes

A klaxon filled Ray's ears. The overlay flashed red all around his peripheral vision: impending disaster. He had his back braced against the computer room's heavy hydraulic door, but he wasn't slowing it down. His feet pushed into the doorframe, and the structure began to press him in half.

Bad time for a memory gap. "Cass! Ando! *Now!*"

"Just one sec—" Ando said, but Cass grabbed him by the back of his shirt and hauled him out of the chair like a rag doll. The door kept moving, and something in Ray's hip gave. He set his hands on the frame to reinforce his futile efforts. Ando leapt over Ray's buckling legs and ran into the corridor. Cass followed, grabbing Ray's arm as she passed, and he stumbled out of the room.

In a single step, Ray realized his legs weren't going to hold him up. His hip, his eye... he wasn't sure which pain was worse now. "Run!" he shouted. "I'm right behind you!"

right behind you

His wife and son were half dragging him down the hallway toward the open exit door. He could hear the drones behind them—four, he could see on the overlay, and the red pulsing border was growing larger.

Why was the exit door open?

"Wait," Ray said. He tried to slow down but found his feet were useless. "Wait! The door. It's—"

the door it's

They were outside, he and Cass, watching Ando run across the building's dimly lit lawn, disappearing into the night, into safety, when the blast wave hit. Still under his arm she was lifted along with him. He tried to pull her in front of him, to shield her from the worst of the blast, but she was gone, abruptly, from his hands, and the red overlay filled his vision, blinding him.

"Cass!" he shouted, as the red flared into white. "Cass!"

And then there was nothing.

He was on his back, unmoving, something roaring around him, deafening.

"Cass? Ando?

All he saw was white.

It's all right. That's not how this ends.

"Dad?"

He's safe. Even groggy, Ray felt relief surge through him. His eyes wouldn't open, but he tried to speak. Something remotely resembling language came out of his mouth.

"It's okay. You're okay."

Wait—this wasn't Ando. This was the voice he'd heard earlier, the one he'd thought was his own. Some of Ray's relief ebbed away.

"Why can't he talk?" the voice asked.

"He's readjusting." A pleasant enough voice, but not deep and warm and husky. Not Cass, then. "His vitals are good. Give him a little time."

Ray felt fingers tuck themselves under his, and he slowly became aware of his body again. Weak, exhausted. His eye still hurt, but his hip ached less than he would have expected, what with having been blown to bits. His hand convulsed on the foreign fingers: they were long, thick, the skin dry and calloused. "Cass.'

The hand gave his a squeeze. "She's gone ahead," the man said. Gentle, soothing. Not a tactic one expected from a government agent. Ray managed to force his eyes open.

He was in a small space surrounded by medical equipment, illuminated by a bright light on the ceiling. An IV bag swung next to his bed. An ambulance, perhaps, though he had no sense of motion. The woman stood at his feet, staring at a screen displaying his vitals. Stout and dark-haired, she was dressed in a matching cotton shirt and pants: a doctor or a nurse.

The man holding his hand, watching him with anxious eyes, had a salt-and-pepper mustache and a well-lined face that Ray could almost, but not quite, place. The hair on his head was black with flecks of silver: tight curls, neatly trimmed. The way Cass always kept her hair.

Easy to look after, she always said. He couldn't remember if he'd ever told her how much he loved it.

"My family," he said to the man, managing to tighten his fingers. So weak, his hand. "Is my family all right?"

Another squeeze from the stranger. Such bright eyes this man had, and something familiar about them. That sharp tilt toward the inside, the way the left eyelid drooped, just a little. Ando had the same eyes. Maybe this man was a relative.

"Your family is fine," the man said.

The voice sounded familiar and thick, but all Ray heard was the reassurance, and when the relief took him again, white and clean and silent, he allowed himself to fall asleep.

"It was the one you wrote for the 65th," Ando told his mother.

He sat on the grass, legs crossed, elbows on his knees. He wasn't sure he'd be able to stand afterward—he'd had a knee replacement at 45—but he could see her better when he was seated. The ground beneath him was cool, but the afternoon sun warmed him even as the breeze chilled the dampness on his cheeks.

"You made me out to be such a brat in that one, you know? But he always liked it. He got to be a hero." Ando laughed. "And you got to ream me out for once. I always wondered why you never did in real life. Lord knows I earned it."

The breeze picked up, and a dried leaf tumbled across his lap.

"For tomorrow, I was thinking of the rocket launch, the one you wrote when I went off to college. It's shorter, but he always loved sitting on top of a ball of exploding fuel. I've been talking to the caseworker, and since it's still a prototype, she thinks they might be able to get us an insurance exception. Maybe even for another two, which, at this point, may be enough. Nobody will say." The words were coming harder now. "They know, but they won't say."

Carefully, Ando unfolded his long limbs and pushed himself to his feet, feeling his spine crack as he rose. That'd be next: a lower lumbar replacement. They were getting better these days, but he hated surgery, no matter how quick the recovery. Still, he needed to be able to sit when he talked to his mother.

"There's so much I wish I could tell you, Mom. But maybe... maybe next time, I'll just write it down."

He leaned down to press his lips against the headstone, just once, before he left her alone in the twilight.

———

... 40%... 85%... 98%... Upload complete. Initiating connection.

———

"Colonel? Ray! Are you *napping?*"

Ray's eyes snapped open at the sound of Cass' voice, and he took a deep breath of the space shuttle's generated oxygen. Before his eyes, the virtual instrument overlay glowed green.

"Negative, CAPCOM," he said. "Just making sure you're paying attention."

The overlay updated the countdown: T-minus 30 seconds. Damn, he'd almost missed it. He lowered his helmet's visor, and the hiss of the capsule's environmental systems grew quieter.

The overlay began counting down: T-minus 10, 9, 8...

"Bring me some stardust, Colonel," CAPCOM said, her voice clear in his ear.

Ray grinned. "You got it, Cass."

The engine ignited with a deafening roar, slamming him back in his seat. But all Ray could hear was his heartbeat, turning the explosion into music, bright and hot and joyous.

SINGLE POINT OF FAILURE

M ercury is going to kill me.

Jaceer was the first, and of course everyone thought it was suicide. She was in the industrial freezer with the meds and the etching solutions, stripped down to her underwear, the safety lock sabotaged from the inside. It's not like the thing is soundproofed, either; if she'd yelled for help we'd have heard her, even in the middle of the goddamned night. Dr. Sofara didn't even bother with an autopsy, just thawed her out, ashed her, and packed her in a box for the next drone home.

I felt bad for her family, but really, she was kind of a bitch.

Not that I let anybody know what I was thinking. Kellan knew it, because even with all the fucked-up shit we've done to each other over the last thirty years, he never stopped being able to read my mind. But in public? I had the big sad eyes and the platitudes, and I attended the Company-sponsored psychological refresher courses along with everybody else.

We had to redistribute her work, of course. No new staff until the resupply ship was due—another 300 days. I have enough of a background in mechanics that I was able to pick up her shift moving the solar collector, but the others had to take over her janitorial tasks. So I wasn't the first one who started trashing her memory out loud.

I didn't tell anybody about the dream.

The dream where I was the one in the freezer, where I'd left my clothes folded neatly on the bed at Kellan's feet. The dream where I stood, patient, waiting for cold to turn to pain to turn to numbness, until that final darkness swallowed all the sorrows of my life.

The dream I had the night before we found her.

Mercury Station sees a lot of suicides, but Kellan and I figured we'd be immune. We'd worked every mine station in the solar system, including five years out by Jupiter and two years on an IndoAsian asteroid trawler. Close quarters like that, years at a time, you see it all: fighting and fucking and even mass murder. The Company writes off the losses and ships you off to the next assignment. Death is old hat at this point.

But Mercury's different. People who've never been here say it's living on the poles, half-underground on a world that either wants to fry you or freeze you, but really it's the weird-ass sense of time you get when everything goes retrograde. Relativity be damned— when objects you think you know start moving the wrong way, reality starts warping, and I'm not talking about wormholes and time dilation.

Einstein was smart, but he didn't know shit about psychology.

Tohan was next. Industrial accident. Cleaning out the dust filters on the primary solar collector, and forgot to put his thermal gloves back on after a break. Fused the fabric of the liners into his skin, and burned his hands down to the bone. Took him three days to die of sepsis, and even though we stuck him in the room furthest away from our sleeping quarters, we could hear him screaming the whole time.

That time I'd dreamed of walking toward the collector in my indoor uniform, my eyes open to the burning sun, blinding me almost instantly before the furnace tore me apart.

My dream was merciful. That's something, I guess.

You sign a full indemnity release when you go to Mercury Station. All the mines require releases, but Mercury's is special. The Company tells you Mercury has a higher incidence of accidents, and you pledge both to lower that incidence and absolve the Company of liability if you can't.

I heard rumors a few years back there were protests on Earth about it, but Kellan and I signed without hesitation. What the fuck did we care if we died on Mercury Station?

Maybe that was just me.

Two hundred and forty-seven days to restaffing, and people started dying more regularly. Bogora: food poisoning. Caliente: overnight air leak in her quarters. Siobhan: injected herself with cleaning fluid instead of allergy meds. All suicides or dumbass accidents, only nobody believed that anymore, even if I was the only one who knew what was behind them.

Dr. Sofara decided the place was haunted, and ended up panicking himself out an airlock. If he'd been on collector duty he'd have burned fast, but outside our polar habitat, he had to suffocate. At least it was quick, or quick enough; anyone who's done any interplanetary travel has been trained not to hold their breath. I'm sure it was painless. More or less.

I hadn't dreamed about that one, so he was probably a legit suicide.

Probably.

After we lost twelve, bringing our staffing down to thirty-six, I told Kellan about the dreams. Even after all these years, all the bitterness and hatred, I still thought he'd comfort me.

He rolled his eyes. "The universe doesn't fucking revolve around you, you know," he said, and walked away.

I knew, then, what I should have known years ago. And I knew what the dreams meant.

Sometimes you stay together only because you said you would, because you made a promise. Because it's the right thing to do. *Loyalty*. And then you've lived your whole life, and loyalty is hollow and starved and meaningless, and there's nothing left for you at all.

Kellan never understood. It was never the others, the ones he looked at the way he used to look at me—decades since I wanted to touch him, since I'd grieved the feeling I'd lost. It wasn't even the acrimony that followed us to every new job, every new attempt to leave our corrosive history behind.

It wasn't Kellan that broke me. It was *time*. Everything's relative, right?

He should've left me. Why didn't he leave me? If he'd left me, I'd've been free.

And I wouldn't have had to kill him.

Kellan's skills always brought us the most profitable deployments. He had twenty-five years' experience with solar collectors, with conditions much more hazardous than Mercury's: hard vacuum, flimsy equipment, no back-up oxygen. He was obsessive about safety. He said that's how he'd lived so long.

So very, very long.

He pounded on the airlock door, his eyes on mine, pissed off and terrified and realizing, at last, that I was done saving him, that all of our sins had come down to this moment, as our transport rolled placidly toward the solar collector and the daylight terminus and the unfiltered sunlight.

"Open the fucking door!" he shouted, easy to hear, because I'd left him oxygen even as I'd sealed him in the airlock without his thermal protection. I could see in his eyes he couldn't quite believe I'd do it, and I wondered how he could know me so well and still know me not at all. He may have been convinced, there at the end, but it happened too fast: his eyes sublimating in his head, just like my own in the dream, his oh-so-thin clothing turning to flame and ash in seconds, his skin blistering and boiling and turning to black before my eyes.

I waited until there was nothing left of him but superheated dust.

By the time the others called to ask why Kellan's telemetry had been interrupted, I'd manufactured a convincing level of hysteria. They really seemed to think I was traumatized.

That left us with twenty-three. And I believed it would finally stop.

Ninety-four days before it was due, the Company pulled the resupply ship. One final message: "The station is being abandoned. Your families will be contractually compensated."

You spend your life traveling through space, you know it's big. You know it's deadly. When that message came through, the seventeen of us left recognized, for the first time, how fucking isolated it was.

Most of the others wrote messages telling the Company to go fuck itself in various creative ways. I wrote a message asking for my compensation to go to Kellan's family. I had no one else.

So many ways to die on an alien world.

Suffocation. Injury.

Freezing, poison, bleeding out.

Fighting. *Stir-crazy*, they used to call it. Manesh, Calla, and Adon all knifed each other to death, apparently over the last pack of frozen corn.

We still worked shifts. How bullshit is that? The Company wouldn't be coming for anything, at least not until long after we were all gone. But we needed the occupation.

I dreamed of clawing out my own eyes, of cutting my wrists, of provoking someone until they took the initiative in my stead.

In the morning it was never me.

I began to be grateful.

Twelve of us left.

I don't sleep anymore. I don't dream. For a few days, that helped, but it doesn't matter now. It's still happening. It's independent, broken away from me, leaving nothing but this demon in my head, telling me I used to be in control.

All demons are liars.

It doesn't take someone every day. I think it likes giving us hope.

We've tried working in pairs, locking ourselves in one big room, chaining ourselves together. It doesn't matter. It gets us anyway.

It doesn't even wait for night anymore.

I don't know how long I've been in this airlock. I brought food, but it's gone now. For an hour. For a day. I don't know.

I can hear the others. Screaming, Crying. Dying? I can't tell. Dying, living—in the end, it's all the same.

The demon still whispers to me, trying to make me sleep, but

I don't. I brought more stims than I did food. Enough stims to kill me long before I run out. I started out judicious with them, but I don't remember when the last dose was, and it's easier just to keep taking them. It's the only way to be sure.

I can't save the others. They bang on the door, they beg me. They want in, or they want out—I don't know. We all speak the same language, but I can't make out their meaning anymore.

I tried, for a while, to tell them there was something here, something that started in my dreams and came to life, inhabiting the halls, feeding off the close heat of the sun and Einstein's madness.

I don't remember what it was like not to be empty. I don't remember what it was like to think this was strange, or painful. I am hollow and hungry and endless, and this is what I have always been.

They bang on the door and beg me, and it doesn't matter. It'll kill them, all of them. It'll kill me, too, someday.

But by God, it'll kill me last.

UNTO DUST

A CENTRAL CORPS SHORT

The night after Tom Foster's wife died, he lay in the bed they used to share and stared at the ceiling, the sporadic hum of late-night shuttle traffic brittle and unreal in his head.

He did not sleep.

The next morning, he listened to his children arguing for more than half an hour before it occurred to him he ought to get out of bed.

He stood, still in the clothes he'd put on the previous morning, the dark trousers and close-fitting jacket that passed for casual teaching attire. He'd had them on less than an hour when the Corps Admiralty comms office had informed him there had been an accident, and he'd known the rest before they said it aloud. He'd worn them taking a shuttle to his daughter's school, and then his son's, to tell them their mother was not coming home this time.

Meg had screamed and howled and beat at his chest, and he'd put his arms around her while she sobbed. Greg had blinked, and said "Are you sure?" as he stood, unmoving, across the room from his father.

It had been so much easier to tell Meg.

Meg, Tom realized, as he walked down the stairs, was doing most of the yelling. *At least that much hasn't changed*, he thought, and then wondered why it would have.

"What do you think people are going to say about you?" Meg was shouting at her brother, who was leaning against the sink, arms crossed, as Tom entered the kitchen. "Your mother *died* yesterday, or don't you remember?"

His daughter, Tom reflected, did not look much like his wife. Where Kate was—had been—fine-featured and delicate, Meg, at seventeen, was more like her father: sharp and frank and handsome in a way that suited her vivid personality. But she had her mother's perfect jet-black curls and dark eyes, and her merciless ability to strike to the heart of any argument.

It was Greg who resembled his mother. At twelve, the boy was already beautiful, with the angular, masculine version of Kate's lovely face. Kate had worried for Greg for years: he had grown tall early, and was already passing for eighteen, even older. People had been giving him things and wanting things from him for years. He was a level-headed boy, and so far hadn't had his head turned by the attention, but Tom knew the older Greg got the more being treated as an adult would become appealing. Tom had discussed the issue with his son, but despite their similar temperaments, Tom never got past the feeling that he wasn't getting through. It was Kate who always knew what to say to Greg, Kate who could make him laugh, think, make the right choices.

"I remember," Greg said to his sister. His voice was low and composed, but his eyes, gray like Tom's, were full of rage.

"If you go to school today you're a *fucking monster*," Meg said, and that shocked Tom out of his silence.

"That's enough, Meg," he said.

Both children looked at him, but only Meg flinched, her gaze defiant. "Dad. He can't go to school today. They'll never stop talking about him if he does. They'll say he didn't love her."

Oh, Meggie. "Meg, honey, can you give us a minute?"

Meg shot her brother a look of triumph, and stomped off up the stairs.

Greg was watching his father with wary eyes. Tom waited until Meg's step had faded in the direction of her bedroom, then took a breath. "I take it you want to go to school."

"I've got a test today," Greg said.

"Could get you excused," Tom offered.

"I don't want to be excused."

Greg had been like this since babyhood. Even then, when something distressed him, the best thing to do was to find him another occupation—not a story or a song, but a task or a puzzle, something he could give his focus and his energy. Something with a solution. Kate had thought it a healthy adaptation. Tom always worried it was avoidance.

"What do you need, Greg?" he asked.

Greg straightened. Nearly Tom's height already; in a year, he'd be taller. "I need to go to school."

After a moment, Tom nodded. "Have some breakfast," he said, "and I'll take you in." He headed for the meal generator, and Greg sat down at the kitchen table.

———

The day after his wife's death, Tom Foster stayed in the house with his daughter.

Meg spent the day railing: against the Corps, against malfunctioning starships, against the Admiralty and all technology. Against her brother, and against her mother for choosing such a risky career, for leaving them when they needed her. She cried and screamed and Tom held her when she allowed it and let her be when she didn't. The only time he interfered was when

Greg came home from school and silently proceeded to his room.

"Let him process it his own way," Tom told her when she moved to go after her brother, and for a little while she was angry with Tom before she began railing against the world again.

That night he slept for nearly half an hour, and dreamt his entire life had been a lie.

The Corps gave him six days before they sent an admiral, a sober-eyed woman called Overton who was nominally Tom's own age. She arrived in his front yard in a small, overpowered shuttle that her inexperienced pilot managed to land on top of a flowering shrub. Tom watched from his front door, squinting into the sun that shone across the surface of the lake as the Admiral and her three escorts extracted themselves from their misplaced transport.

"If you'd commed first," he told her, once they'd come up the stairs onto the porch, "I could've told you how to land without flattening my garden."

His tone, he suspected, was not terribly friendly, but Overton seemed used to such receptions. "May we come in, Mr. Foster?" she asked.

"That's Professor," he corrected her. "And *you* can come in. *They* can wait out here."

All three members of her entourage wore ensign's insignias, uniforms pristine and unwrinkled, faces professional masks. One of them was pale and pasty, and at his words a flush of color climbed up from her neckline and over her small-chinned, round face. That she didn't otherwise move was an impressive feat of discipline. *I should be more hospitable*, he thought, but after Admiral Overton stepped into his house, he let the door slide closed behind her.

Overton had stopped inside the door and was surveying his living room, her eyes straying over the windows and past the stairs into the open kitchen. She was a compact woman, short and rigid, with a square, tan face, wide forehead, and unexpectedly delicate nose. Her expression was grim but relaxed, and it was only her eyes, dark and watchful, that betrayed how alert she was. He suspected, if he asked her, she could tell him without looking again exactly how many glasses he'd left on the kitchen counter.

"I'd offer you something," he said, walking around her toward the sink, "but I don't want you to stay." He began picking up glasses.

"I appreciate your candor." Tom didn't turn around, and he heard her step closer. "I'm very sorry about your wife, Professor Foster."

He should have let the ensigns in and left the admiral on the porch. "Your people have already sent that message," he told her. "So why don't you tell me why you're really here."

"I'm here to give my condolences." She sounded a little surprised. "And to make sure your family has what they need."

There it was. "If I told you what my family needs is for you to stay away," he asked, "would you honor that?"

She was silent, and he turned at last. She was regarding him with shrewd eyes, calculating, trying to figure out how to handle him.

He wondered, for a moment, how far he'd get if he went for her throat. All Corps officers were trained in hand-to-hand, and Tom was only a teacher; still, he had height and weight on her, and that might at least give him a head start.

"Shall we be honest, Admiral?" he said.

"By all means."

"I know you're watching my son. I know you've always been watching my son."

"We watch anyone who's got interest and aptitude," she said.

"My wife worked for you people for *twenty years*, so don't talk to me like I'm naive," he snapped. "You've got thirty kids sector-wide, maybe two hundred in the whole galaxy, with Greg's level of *aptitude*. You've been hovering his whole goddamned life, waiting to get your claws into him." He took a step forward and indulged his need for violence by towering over her. "*Now is not the time.*"

She didn't even flinch. "The Corps looks after our own," she said. "Doctor Leburu had an exemplary career. It's our duty to look after her family."

"It was your *duty* to keep her alive."

It wasn't true. He knew it when he said it. It was an argument he'd had with Kate over and over again: how could she pledge her life to the Corps when she had two children? What the hell was wrong with her priorities?

But Overton let it pass. "Regardless, Professor, we're not here today to address aptitude. We're here to offer our services to anyone in your family who may need them."

"Like my son?"

"If he wants to talk."

"Oh, it's *talking* you're offering." Tom knew a few Corps counselors. They were highly trained, and for the most part deeply compassionate people; but not a single soldier, up to and including his wife, ever saw them as anything but an irritating hurdle to be cleared after a bad day. "You'd talk to me, then."

"If you'd find it helpful."

Not fucking likely. "And my daughter."

"She enjoys chemistry, I'm told."

He waited a moment for the heat behind his eyes to subside. "I'm not sure it's sensible, Admiral, for you to let on that you're watching my daughter as well."

She gave him a thin smile. "Your daughter isn't going to be enlisting any time soon."

"If you know that," he told her, "you know that nobody in this house is interested in talking to your Corps counselors."

"Are you sure about that?"

"Of course."

They looked at each other, and her expression didn't change as she waited. When she nodded and turned to go, it should have felt like victory. "Should you change your mind, Professor," she said, as she made her way to the door.

He wanted her out of his house. He wanted her out of his memory.

She opened the door, and immediately he heard voices: three unfamiliar, no doubt her escort, and his son's, already nearly as deep as an adult's. Greg sounded interested, engaged, animated; startled, Tom heard the boy laugh.

As Overton stepped through the door, the three Corps soldiers came to attention, and Greg's face turned into a mask. Tom, who knew his child, could see the combination of embarrassment and resentment in Greg's eyes.

"Get in the house, son," he said. Tom kept his tone mild, but Greg knew him, too, and for a moment Tom thought the boy would defy him. But instead Greg straightened, took a moment to nod at Overton's escort, and sauntered into the house as if he were leaving of his own accord.

Some days Tom wished for more cracks in his son's aplomb.

"I don't want to see you here again," Tom said to Admiral Overton. He met the eyes of each member of her escort, one after another; the pale woman blotched scarlet again. "I don't want to see any of you anywhere on my property. Is that understood?"

"Of course. We've no desire to bother you." Her next word was a sharp command: "Company!" All four of them in unison saluted Tom.

A gesture of courtesy, for the family of the dead.

Those ensigns are children, he told himself. *Twice Greg's age. Maybe not even. They don't understand.* He kept his eyes on Admiral Overton, and he said, "Stay away from my family."

He knew she could hear the threat in his voice, could hear he meant it. But all she did was incline her head at him, and say, "As you wish."

He stayed on the porch long after her shuttle had vanished across the sunlit lake.

———

Eight nights after Tom Foster's wife died, the reality of it all came crashing down on his head.

Never again. Never again her hair curled around his fingers, the smell of her sweat, the silk of her fine skin, the warmth of her body against his. Never again her musical voice, so often harsh during the fights he would always lose, because he loved her and she knew it and he'd impale himself on a hundred knives to keep her happy. Never again that sense of peace when she came home, that sense of rending when she left. Never again the plans for the future, when Greg and Meg would be grown and they would be at long last alone again, just the two of them, as it had been in the beginning when they were young and full of hope and everything was yet to come.

Never again.

He prowled the house as quietly as he could, unable to stand still, unable to focus on anything. He wanted to get out, to run down to the lake, to scream and let his agony be swallowed by the waves; but upstairs were his children, and they needed him. He'd always been their first line of defense, even when they were little, before Kate had resumed active duty and allowed herself to be taken away. He couldn't leave them now, never mind the gaping void that was his heart.

"Dad?"

Tom had been bending over the kitchen sink, hyperventilating, a great weight over his chest preventing him from inhaling. At Greg's voice the weight eased, and he was able to turn around and be something resembling a father.

His son stood there, in his pajama bottoms. Greg was still little-boy skinny, but he was starting to develop some definition in his biceps. He'd let his hair grow too long again; it grew straight out, and when he slept it became misshapen, flat on one side and askew on the other. Tom had tamed his own wiry hair into long locs decades ago, but he'd always suspected his son would choose short hair, like his mother's, like they favored in the Corps.

"You all right, Greg?" Tom asked.

Greg was frowning. The frown took over his whole face, from his forehead to his eyebrows to his expressive mouth. The look was already intimidating; Tom thought Greg might find it useful someday. Only those who knew the boy well understood the look meant not anger, but concentration.

"I was going to ask you that," Greg said.

"Of course I am," Tom said reflexively. He braced a hand against the kitchen counter and straightened. He realized, abruptly, that his face was wet; he didn't remember crying. "Of course. I just couldn't sleep. I couldn't sleep." Why couldn't he stop talking? "I couldn't—"

"Dad." Greg's voice had gone soft, and he took a step forward. "Dad. It's okay."

"I couldn't sleep," he said again, and this time he noticed when the tears started. "Greg. I'm so sorry. I couldn't sleep."

His legs couldn't hold him, then, and his knees hit the kitchen floor, and he kept stammering but there were no words anymore. And without hesitation his reticent, angry son knelt on the floor before his father and put his skinny arms around him, and Tom sobbed and sobbed as Greg rubbed his back and said "It's okay, Dad. It's okay."

Fourteen days after his wife's death, Tom went to a bar.

Tom never enjoyed going to bars on his own. Drinking wasn't

one of his great pleasures; he did not get drunk easily, and he was mostly indifferent to the taste. Kate liked to drink. They would go out together, and she would get tipsy and affectionate and silly, and sometimes crawl into his lap in public, never mind they were both over forty and too serious for such behavior at the best of times. When they got home he would bundle her up in his arms—she was tall but slim, and she folded up against his chest like she was built to fit there—and carry her to their bedroom. As often as not she would fall immediately asleep, and he would lie next to her and watch her breathe, content beyond imagining.

Meg always rolled her eyes when she caught her parents flirting, but she had told him once that as much as it embarrassed her it also made her happy.

This bar was open-air, an optimistic setup for Otter Lake in the fall, but somehow the place survived season after season. It had avoided, over decades, the sporadic trend of full automation and survived swapping one taciturn bartender for another. Tom didn't remember this one, a sturdy, efficient woman of indeterminate age, but she brought him two fingers of scotch without his asking, and set it down before him just as he sat next to his friend.

Bob Hastings had two empty glasses in front of him, and was most of the way through a third. By the look of him, he'd been well on his way before the first of those glasses had arrived.

Tom nursed his own drink, feeling the comforting burn down his throat, the slight loosening in his limbs. He had thought, more than once in the last two weeks, of coming here and doing what Bob seemed to be doing: drinking for as long as he was able to stay upright, and then drinking some more. He was not sure there was a reasonable conclusion to that path.

"You look like hell," Tom said at last.

Bob Hastings almost never looked like hell. He was a little older than Tom, with a slighter build but far more muscle. Tom was not one to notice male beauty, but he'd seen enough people stop and stare at Bob Hastings to know that the man's sculpted face and brilliant blue eyes held a nearly universal appeal. Usually those eyes were filled with good humor, and occasionally light cynicism, but not now. Tom had known Bob for twelve years, and knew the man was far more soft-hearted than he cared to let on to most of the world.

He was also the only other person alive who understood what Tom was going through.

Bob put down his empty glass and caught the bartender's eye again. "That's because I've been drunk for two weeks."

"Impressive," Tom remarked.

"I keep waiting for it to kill me," Bob confided. "So far, no luck."

Tom took another sip. "This stuff's too good. You should try distilling your own."

"I did that once. Took me a month to get anything decent. Inefficient." The bartender returned, and Bob started in on the new drink. "Which one did they send?"

"Overton," Tom told him.

Bob snorted. "They knew you were pissed off."

They had known he was pissed off since the day he and Kate met. "How much do I have to worry about this?" he asked.

Bob considered. "Sending Overton means they want your good will," he said.

"That cold-hearted ice age cyborg?"

"If they'd wanted to railroad you," Bob reminded him, "they'd have sent someone like Turay who would have given you some bullshit about politics and new frontiers and supporting what Katie loved, that kind of manipulative shit. They know you prefer a straight shooter."

It was Tom's turn to snort. "Not an admiral in that outfit wouldn't point the gun right on target and still hit themselves in the ass."

"Yeah, but Overton's the closest. She spouts the bullshit, but she doesn't try to make it what it isn't. You throw her out?"

"Yep."

"She give you any trouble?"

"No." Which wasn't precisely true. He told Bob what he'd found when he left the house. "I don't know what to do with Greg," he confessed. "He holds it all so close. He doesn't talk about anything. He's focusing on his routine, and I guess sticking with what he knows is helping. But—" Tom remembered his son's laugh. "There's so much in his head, Bob, and I've never been able to get at it. That was always Kate. Now..."

He fell silent, and he drank, and Bob drained another glass. They were quiet for a long time.

"I'm not sure I'm the best person to talk to him," Bob said at last.

"He knows I've always hated the Corps. You're qualified, and you're one of them. That gives you more leverage than I've got."

"I'm not sure I'm the best person to give him the *this is how you go on when someone you love dies* speech."

"Then don't give him that speech." Tom looked over at him. "Just...he needs to talk to someone, and he won't talk to me. He might talk to you. Will you try?"

Bob met Tom's eyes, and for an instant the agony Tom saw there was so much a mirror of his own he thought he would collapse.

"Everyone says he's so much like Katie," Bob said. "Not just how he looks. His ambitions. His temper. They're wrong, you know. He's just like you."

"That's why I can't get in."

At last, Bob nodded his head. "I'll talk to him," he promised. "I'll try."

A breeze blew in over the lake, and Tom smelled that stagnant tang the water took on when they were overdue for rain. When he finally asked, "What happened, Bob?" he was almost sure he was ready to hear the answer.

Bob's reflexive bravado failed, and he became suddenly everything Tom felt himself: ancient, bewildered, lost and grieving. "The official story," Bob said. "is that the drive blew when they tried to initiate the field."

"I heard the official story. I want to know *what happened*."

"All I have is rumor."

"What about the flight recorder?"

"They haven't got it."

Tom turned to stare at him. "You're telling me an engine explosion is enough to destroy a Corps-manufactured flight recorder?"

"Nope."

He studied the bottom of his glass, and Tom waited.

"I get away with a lot of shit, you know," Bob said. "Always have. Since I was a kid. Makes me an asshole, I think." He put the glass down, and this time he didn't signal the bartender for another. "Katie never let me get away with shit. Not once. Not from the day I met her."

Tom inhaled patience. "She trusted you," he said. "Maybe five people in her whole life, including me, that she trusted."

"I should've taken that assignment."

"They didn't offer it to you," Tom pointed out. "And if she wasn't going to give it up for her kids, why do you think she'd have given it up for you?" *I don't need you getting rootbound in your own guilt.*

"I loved her, you know."

"We've had this conversation. Now stop being a maudlin fucking drunk and tell me *what happened to my wife*."

Bob inhaled, then exhaled, then nodded to the bartender. "When I say it's all rumor," he said, "I don't mean *rumor we all know is truth* rumor. I mean *rumor*. Rumor that's honest to God no more than speculation. All I do know is that it wasn't a fucking engine explosion, because that's bullshit on its face." He rubbed a hand through his hair. "Some people are saying Andy Kelso went crazy and blew the ship himself."

"I've heard that one." Tom had dismissed it immediately. Kate would have known if her captain was that unstable.

"There's also the rumor of aliens."

Everyone wanted aliens to exist, and in nearly a thousand years of exploring the galaxy, no one had found a shred of evidence that they did. "They've sent probes into that wormhole for decades," Tom said. "You're telling me it took the *Phoenix* doing a fly-by to attract alien attention? Please."

"And then," Bob said, "there's the rumor that the wormhole spat something out."

Tom looked over, but Bob wouldn't meet his eyes. "You think there's something to that one."

Bob shrugged; as drunk as he was, the gesture was graceless. "You got me, Tom. They picked up all kinds of crazy readings after the explosion; but that place is going to be irradiated for forty years. Nothing they're picking up is reliable yet. It'll be five years at least before they can even verify the size of the blast."

"But you think that's what happened."

This time it was Bob's turn to be introspective. "I think," he said at last, "that I don't want it to be an accident. That I don't want to have lost her to some bullshit engine overload glitch that should have been designed out of our starships twenty years ago. That I want there to be *something* to come out of it, some reason she didn't die for nothing."

"Everybody dies for nothing," Tom said.

Tom knew Bob Hastings well enough to understand why the man started to laugh.

"Say that again, son?"

Greg straightened, his eyes shifting toward the wall. "I'm going to quit the Corps prep program."

Three weeks after his wife was killed, Tom Foster had been in his living room, scrolling through an inbox flooded with nightmarish condolences and bureaucratic nonsense around Kate's death, when his children came home from school together. That in itself was suspicious; Meg, five years older than her brother, generally wanted nothing to do with Greg in public. What was even more suspicious was that she looked anxious, and a little pleased, and was hovering over Greg as if he were a much smaller child.

And Greg was putting up with it.

At her brother's words, Meg met Tom's eyes, and she looked so hopeful and hungry for approval that if he'd had any heart left it would have broken.

I guess it's time for me to start parenting again.

"Meg, sweetheart," he said, giving her a gentle smile, "can you let your brother and I talk for a bit?"

"Of course." She reached out and rubbed Greg's arm, encouraging, approving, and headed up the stairs.

Tom waited until he heard her door close.

"This her idea?" Tom asked.

Greg shook his head. "I've been thinking about it for a while now."

Tom suspected if he'd been eavesdropping more on his children he'd have found Meg working long and hard to plant the thought in her brother's head. "Why do you want to quit?"

At that Greg met Tom's eyes, just for a moment, and Tom caught confusion and uncertainty. *He thought I'd approve*, Tom realized. *He thought I'd jump at this.* "It's not the only thing there is," Greg said.

"So what do you think you'll do?"

Greg shifted from foot to foot. "I could teach. Like you do."

Definitely Meg's idea. "You'd make a fine teacher, I'm sure," Tom said, and he meant it. Greg had both charm and patience when he chose, and he seemed reasonably good at breaking down ideas into simpler components. "Why do you want to teach?"

And with one shrug, Greg was a little boy again. "It's a good job," he said. "It's important."

"Lot of things are important."

"It's here," Greg said. "I could, I don't know. Stay close by."

Aha. "To take care of me."

"Why not?"

There was an edge of resentment to Greg's statement, the beginnings of a teenaged separation that Tom had long suspected was going to be hell on them both. Meg had led Greg to expect he'd be rewarded for this move, that he'd have Tom's gratitude, that he could join his sister in becoming caretakers for their father, so abruptly all alone.

Meg he'd have to deal with later, and there would be yelling and recriminations and her uncanny ability to slip a verbal dagger between his ribs. Her mother's daughter, indeed. But before him was Greg, twelve going on forty, trying to figure out what his life of service was supposed to look like now that the Corps had killed his mother.

It's never been about the Corps, Tom wanted to say to him. *Even for your mother, it was never about the Corps. It was about being out there, the wonder, the unknown. The adventure. Even helping people, even the catastrophic rescues—that all came second. She went out there because she had to, because it fed her soul like nothing else in her life, not me, not Meg, not you. You could have told her it would take her life someday. You could even have told her when and how. And she wouldn't have stopped. Do you see it, son? If she couldn't stay for you, she couldn't stay. And you can't stay for me.*

Tom leaned back on the sofa and looked up at his son. "If teaching is what you want, that's one thing," he said. "But if you give up your dream out of some misguided idea that it's what I want, or what Meggie wants, or for any reason other than it's stopped being your dream, I'll put you out of this house and you can sacrifice all your hard work for someone else. You understand?"

Greg grew very still, and Tom watched his face: irritation, then anger, then embarrassment. And finally, definitively, relief. He didn't smile, but his eyes lit up in a way Tom hadn't seen since the last time Kate was home.

"What about Meg?" Greg asked.

"You let me take care of your sister."

"She's going to be mad at me."

"Yeah, she is. But she needs to follow her dreams, too, Greg. And it's my job to make sure she feels she can do that."

A look of understanding passed between the two of them, and then Greg started bouncing on his toes. "Do I have time for a run before dinner?" he asked.

"If you run fast."

At that, Greg flashed a grin, and he turned and dashed out the front door, all child once again.

———

Four weeks after his wife died, Tom watched his son leave the house to visit Bob Hastings, Lieutenant Commander, Central Corps Medical, to talk about losing his mother.

Tom pretended he didn't know where Greg was going.

THINKING INSIDE THE BOX

"Power variance nominal," says Bunny.

I glance up at her face through the power room window. She's bathed in light, that strange, nearly sub-visual shade of blue-violet some techie centuries ago decided should mean "nothing's happening but nothing's fucked up." Her eyes are on the panel in front of her, and I relax a little. Bunny's attention span isn't a given, what with her being bugfuck insane, but most days she's good enough at her job.

I'm not allowed in the power room yet. I've only been on The Box Starstation three months, and I'm still stuck in Monitoring, this tiny room that'd feel a lot more comfortable without the floor-to-ceiling glass showing me unobstructed light years of star-studded pitch-black fuck-all. Bunny's supposed to be training me, but she doesn't really have an aptitude for teaching. Her instructions come in the form of handing me tech manuals at breakfast while she's humming and swaying her way around the cramped kitchen, as if one of us isn't real.

Days I'm pretty sure it's me.

"Proceed to Contact," I say, and Bunny slides her finger across the panel.

Somewhere inside The Box, some bastard who spent too much damn money for a ticket is getting a fast-forward showing of the rest of his life.

I know what you're thinking: Nobody cares about The Box anymore. Most people think it's over, a fad that died an ignominious death. I mean, that's fair. A 30 percent rate of irreversible insanity is the kind of thing you could expect to kill an exotic tourist destination like The Box, and it nearly did. That's why there's only three of us staffing the starstation now —me, Bunny, and Godot, the supervisor—instead of the twenty-seven scientists and industry wankers who camped out here in the middle of Galactic Nowhere for the first fifteen years.

Tourism has dropped off a cliff, for sure; but there are still shitbags stupid enough to believe that if they spend their life savings, The Box is going to tell them their future is full of sunshine and fucking roses.

I thought the same of my future when I was sixteen, before one of my dumbass Lukos highs turned into felony murder. I didn't even do the shooting, but Mattie handed me the gun while the metrodome cops were landing on the roof, and I took it. Lukos makes you fucking stupid. Pled guilty at the advice of my court-appointed advocate, who told me I'd be out young enough to start over; instead they locked me up for life. So maybe it wasn't the Lukos after all.

Prison sucks, no question, but to be honest it wasn't a whole lot worse than pissing away my life robbing the local Smoke-n-Shoot to finance the next high. At least I got free food, and— after the first few years, at least—a reputation as the guy you leave the fuck alone. By forty years in, I was pretty comfortable with the routine. You'd told me a year ago I'd take work out at The Box, I'd've said you were high yourself.

But since the riots on Iobe, the prisons have been overflowing, sometimes with real criminals. Before, I knew exactly how much hardware to roll up in my towel in case I got jumped heading to the showers. After, it turned into a fucking war zone.

The warden and I weren't friendly, but I was an easy prisoner from the start. Kept to myself. Not one to shake things up, me. Once or twice a year, the warden found a way to express gratitude for my temperament. This time, he offered me The Box.

The proposal they give you is simple: A two-year stint on staff at The Box Starstation. Deep space, no visitors, no chatter with anyone but the tourist transports. Not even a fucking letter home. But if you get through your two with a clean record, you're free, full stop. No money, no resources, but your record's expunged, and you can try for paying work.

Assuming you can find anything you can do after being inside. Prison's never been much of a jobs program.

Wasn't thinking about money when I said yes, though. Was thinking about being out. Sunshine. Maybe fresh air. Fuck it, I'd live under a fucking skylane and freeze to death the first night if it meant breathing something non-generated again.

"Contact complete," Bunny says, and she turns to meet my eyes and smiles. It's the smile of a kid ready to clap to show she believes in fairies. Seems Bunny's having one of her bad days.

One of the perks of working at The Box is you can make Contact for free. Often as you want. It's in the contract. Thought about it, on that four-month trip out here, working for passage in the ship's data dungeon. How bad could it be, to see what the rest of my life was going to be like? Can't be any fucking worse than what's come before, right?

I asked Godot, that first night, what the deal was with Bunny. He looked at me and said, "She tried it."

Decided mystery wasn't so bad after all.

The lights in the power room turn back to ordinary prison-shower yellow, and Bunny opens the door. She's pretty, or at least I think she is; at my age anyone under forty years old is fucking Aphrodite. She's tall, but small-boned and thin, and she has this sort of tawny skin that goes all gold in the crappy light. Back when I thought about girls, I'd have let myself go stupid over her, but now I mostly want to be her fucking dad and make sure she eats properly and goes to bed on time.

I wish a lot I'd met Bunny before Contact. I don't think my Bunny is much like the person she was before The Box.

"You had dinner?" I ask her. Behind us, on the other side of the power room, I can hear Godot talking to the client in that low, modulated voice of his that I'm pretty sure is the only reason he's employed here. It's the same crap every time, about disorientation and perspective and how we don't really know for sure that everything The Box shows us is real, so maybe don't panic if it said your life is going to end fucking horribly or fucking soon.

Bunny's already humming, but she answers me. "I ate before." She turns around and walks backward, still next to me, her eyes on the open door to the power room, toward Godot and the client. "That one won't go mad," she tells me, and because Bunny almost never tells me shit, I'm curious.

"How do you know?"

"Godot likes him," she says.

After three months, I'm starting to be able to decode some of Bunny's shorthand. "You mean he's really fucking rich." When she nods, I ask, "Does that make a difference?"

Her hum turns into an affirmative noise. "They think they can change it."

I don't need to understand shorthand for that. Rich people never think life is ever going to fuck them, no matter what. "Which ones go mad?"

She's still walking backward, but she stops humming, and when she looks me in the eye she looks sane enough to make me nervous. "The ones who realize they can't."

Then she smiles, sanity forgotten, and part of me expects her to start clapping her hands.

I was already inside when The Box was discovered. Even with restricted news we heard about it: a chunk of abandoned alien technology, found by a seriously dumbass scientist who thought he'd just hook himself up to it. Four days afterward he did nothing but write, all longhand, without sleeping. Turned out to be just a part of what The Box had shown him: detailed events of the next three years of his life. Week by week the news reported a tally of what The Box had right, and at first it was exciting, like a game of chance. We bet on it, because we were so bored we'd gamble on clipping our fucking toenails, but after the first week folks started getting spooked and dropping out.

The Box was never wrong, not about a single thing that scientist wrote down.

I didn't think much about it, what with still resenting the fuck out of the fundamental injustice of my situation, but I kept on gambling until news on The Box went dark, nearly three years after that scientist first published his results. Learned months later he'd deleted all his papers, transferred his property to some random warehouse worker he'd never met, and took a walk off a skyscraper.

At that point we all started gambling on how long it'd take them to clean up the stain the guy left behind, pulverized bone and organs spread over a forty-meter radius, but I remember this one kid, younger than me even, who wouldn't have anything to do with it. He was hard, all knots and cynicism, and a month later he was transferred to maximum; but that day he was real quiet until dinner when he interrupted our tasteless fucking jokes by saying, "We're not meant to know."

Which made us all laugh. "You don't actually believe that shit, do you?"

I'll never forget that kid's eyes: deep gray like a dead ocean, usually full of confidence and violence and fuck-the-world-ness. He looked at us one after the other, and he said, "All of this? Set before you were born. You really want to know what happens next?"

I laughed with the rest of them, and he went back to being an asshole. But I never forgot that question.

I wonder how long Bunny thought about it before she hooked herself up.

Been a long time since I've slept really well. Not because of prison —you learn fast how to get people to leave you alone or you don't survive. But they say the body needs less sleep when you get older, which must mean I'm fucking ancient, because I can't get more than four hours anymore. Something about missing the sun. Fucks with your brain. We're evolved for sunshine, that unique Sol spectrum. I hear some folks on Earth can't even cope with shorter days.

But it's way before four hours when I wake up.

For three of us, The Box Starstation is fucking luxurious. My room, Bunny's room, Godot's room. The other former staff rooms have been converted for clients to sleep off Contact or—if they've paid—stay for a few days. Besides quarters there's the power room, Monitoring, a small kitchen that doubles as a med center, and a room containing The Box itself. My room is next to The Box room.

Bunny was weird about that when I arrived, and I had to learn about her bugfuck craziness before I understood she was worried about me sleeping so close to it. I like it, though. Both she and Godot are superstitious, which means they never wander down my way, and I get some quiet. You'd think after forty years inside quiet would freak me out, but I love it. I'd inject it like Lukos if I could.

Tonight it's not quiet. There are sounds, metal on metal, as if someone's shoving things around on a table top. And there are tiny human noises, little squeaks, as if someone is trying to swallow a cry.

None of my business. Godot and Bunny have been here a long time. Tech controllers like me come and go. They have each other: the one who sees fairies in the starshine, and the one who kisses paying client ass. You have to rely on *someone* out here in the middle of fucking nowhere.

There's another sound, as if something's been knocked onto the floor, and this time I get up.

Most people don't know The Box isn't an actual box. It's some weird-ass irregular polyhedron, and I guess symmetry is a human thing because it has none. It's as high as my knee, more or less, and I don't think anybody's ever done anything to it since Doctor Skyscraper all those years ago hooked up an AI prosthetic to the maze of alien-ass wires coming out of the thing. The wires aren't copper or fiber or anything I know, and all Bunny's tech manuals say about them is DO NOT TOUCH THE WIRES. Like I'm a fucking idiot.

They built a room around it, and then the starstation. There's a chair for clients to sit while it tells them their futures, and the space is kept comfortably warm. Clients can choose music, too, if they want; some of them paid all the fucking money they had to get here, so why not?

Godot logged the client out six hours ago. There should be nobody in The Box room. But when I approach the door, the sounds get louder, and the human noises don't sound so tiny anymore.

I stop and shrink against the wall, then peer around the doorframe.

Godot's face is visible through the window into the power room, only he's not watching the panel. He's staring at Bunny, who's in the Contact chair, and she's naked with the AI piece on her head and a fucking gag in her mouth while she goes rigid over and over like she's getting electroshock. Against the opposite wall is the client, and his pants are on the floor but he's still wearing some custom-made non-wrinkle silk shirt and he's got his dick in his hand, and every time she moans he jerks harder, and while I'm standing there Godot hisses over the intercom "Keep quiet, you crazy bitch. If you wake the old man, I'll fucking kill you."

Oh, Godot. Not if I see you first.

But it's Bunny who sees me, who meets my eyes with her mad ones, and I didn't think you could see anything when you were in Contact, but what the fuck, Bunny's special. And when she's sure I'm looking back, she shakes her head once, twice: *No.*

The client braces himself against the wall and yells, and Godot doesn't have the balls to tell him to keep it down, and this rich asshole must not do this much because he's sloppy as a teenager about it, and some stunned part of me is wondering who gets to clean the fucking floor. When he's done, his dick is limp and curled like a slug, and I think there are five or six pairs of wire cutters in the kitchen that could take care of that pretty fucking fast.

Bunny keeps staring at me, and she shakes her head *no* again, and through the window Godot looks down at the controls. A moment later, The Box shuts down, and Bunny convulses and passes out.

No. No to what?

Godot steps into the room to personally hand the client his pants, his usual obsequious grin on his face. I back up and head for my room.

Not one to shake things up, me.

Bunny and I have breakfast together.

I want to ask her about the night before, but she's in full humming mode, and she hands me the power room manual. "You need to test on that in a week," she tells me, and smiles. She leaves the room backwards, seeing fairies again, passing Godot as he enters as if he were unimportant scenery. He doesn't bother looking at me, but heads to the cabinet for his usual cereal.

The thing about prison is you get a lot of time to practice. Nearly anything, really. They had a piano in our cell block, and damned if some of the guys weren't too bad. But it was easier if you were practicing something that didn't need outside supplies. Most of my practice was self-defense, but I got too good too fast, and I got bored. So I started learning offense as well.

Forty years is a long fucking time.

I've got an arm around Godot's neck before he even thinks to drop his cereal, and I learn I had him right on this at least: he knows fuck-all about fighting. I can feel his throat working under my forearm, and I tighten my grip, holding the point of a pair of wire cutters under his jaw, right where the nice soft bits are. "What the fuck are you doing to Bunny?" I ask him, because it seems more reasonable to let him try to justify himself before I have him bleed out in our common kitchen.

He makes a squawk, and I loosen my grip just enough for him to be able to rasp out "—her idea! First day we got here! I do it, too, I swear!"

Which is some bullshit. I'd bet my papers out of here Godot's never been in Contact. "Difference is," I growl in his ear, "you're not *fucking nuts*."

"I give her the money, for fuck's sake!" He struggles a little, and I tighten my grip. "You think I'm forcing her into it? Ask her, dammit!"

Fuck if I don't believe him. And fuck if I don't think about Bunny, watching her own life over and over again, layer over layer over layer of bullshit.

I put my mouth closer to his ear. "But that would require me not to kill you right here and now." I mean, fuck. I'm serving life for murder already. They owe me a corpse.

"No! No! Wait!" He manages to sound frantic even though there's nothing but weak puffs of air coming out of him. "You want a cut? Fine, you can have the money! I have enough anyway! You won't even have to do anything for it!"

I knocked a guy out once in prison. Didn't mean to, but the shitbag kept coming at me, and eventually I just held on to him until he dropped. I could drop this fucker, too, and decide later whether to kill him. Assuming I didn't make an unfortunate mistake and crush his windpipe, or accidentally snip his carotid with my wire cutters.

"You're lucky," I tell him. "You won't make nearly as big of a mess as Doctor Skyscraper."

And then something heavy hits the back of my head, and everything goes dark.

dark
dark and
bright and warm and red
blood
against the floor the walls my hands my arm
those wire cutters in her hands as she takes his fingers off
humming
pretty so pretty so kind
even crazy she's so kind to me and i want to save her and
she takes off his shoes and it's his toes this time
less blood because his heart his heart has stopped his heart
my heart
my heart is beating so fast so hard and i am alive not my blood i am alive
and she hums
and she smiles at me
and there are so many so many so
young and old and pain and war and
love and
hearts so many so many hearts i am full i am dying i am coming apart
everything is bright, fire, heat, consumption, apocalypse

and when the flame dies when the flame dies
when it dies
i take a breath free and clear in the sunshine

Contact leaves you with one hell of a hangover.

I'm on an unfamiliar floor, flat on my back, blinking out at the stars, millions of specks of bright dust against that soul-swallowing nothingness. My breath sounds deep and heavy in my ears, and I struggle to sit up, only to find I'm wearing something heavy and stiff that makes it hard to move. On the wall opposite that window to the stars I see the words WARNING: DO NOT OPEN WHEN LIGHT IS RED.

I'm in the fucking airlock.

"Hey!" I yell, and my voice sounds flat and echoes close to my head, and I realize I've got a full helmet on. All dressed up for a trip outside into the fucking vacuum. "*Hey!*"

I hear her humming, then, and it's the same tune I heard when I was in Contact. I press myself against the interior window, so small I can't see much, and when the faceplate bounces off the door I remember I was fucking unconscious, because my head starts to throb in a deeply unpleasant fashion.

When my vision clears, I see The Box, and on the floor in front of it is Godot, lying on the floor staring at me, only not really. His eyes are wide and unblinking and starting to look a little desiccated, and I wonder how long I was out, how long he's been dead. His head seems to have sunk below floor level, but after a moment I realize that's because his skull has been bashed into pudding and is oozing out onto the metal plating. Even so, she couldn't have killed him here; there isn't nearly enough blood. I blink once, and things are blurry, but when I blink again I look down at his hands.

Those wire cutters left clean wounds.

Bunny is behind The Box, and I can see all those alien wires lying on the floor, disconnected, even though I can't see what she's doing. She must have heard me bash into the door, but she doesn't look up, doesn't acknowledge my presence at all.

"You put me in Contact, didn't you?" I ask. When she doesn't answer, I add, "Just guessing, because I've had concussions before and this was way fucking weirder than they were."

She still says nothing,

"I'm not crazy,"

The humming stops. "No."

Relaxed and tranquil, like there isn't a dead guy in the floor with no fingers and toes. "Is that a myth, then? That people go crazy?"

"No," she says again. She hasn't looked up, and I still can't see what she's doing. "The myth is why."

I don't know what the fuck that means.

"What are you doing?" She doesn't answer, just starts humming again, and I claw at the airlock controls, but even though the LIGHT is not RED I can't do a fucking thing in these vacuum gloves, and my sluggish fingers can't even yank them off. Maybe I can knock the door down with this smooth-ass helmet. "Godot was a dick, Bunny. I say we flush him with the rest of the organic waste, scrub the place down, and tell them he took a wrong turn one night and sucked vacuum. Nobody's going to miss that ratfucker, not even his own mother."

But it seems Bunny's not interested in Godot's grieving relatives. She sits back from her work, still humming, and cocks her head to one side, looking it over. After a moment she gets her feet under her and stands, looking past me at something on the other side of the room. Stepping over Godot like he's a wrench someone forgot to put away, she heads into the power room.

I watch as she bends over the console, and the light dims to that fucking useless blue. "What are you doing?" I shout, but she won't fucking answer me. I see her hands moving, swift and sure, and after a moment the light turns from blue to red.

"Bunny?"

"Airlock cycle initiated," says the station voice calmly.

Jesus fuck, she's going to space me. "Bunny!" I start pounding on the door. "I won't tell anyone! You know I won't! Let me out of here!"

Bunny leaves the power room, stepping over Godot again, and walks up to the door, staring at me through the small window. I hear a klaxon begin to sound, and the station voice says, "Power overload. Automatic shutdown failed. Please initiate manual shutdown." And all at once, I put it together.

Bunny doesn't want to kill me.

"You don't need to die," I say, looking down at her through the window. She's so small, and her face holds such innocence. I have no idea what crime she committed to end up in the system, what favor she did to get a ticket here. Maybe she's some kind of killer revolutionary or some over-idealistic rich kid from Iobe. Maybe everything she's ever done for me was faked, but I don't think so. I don't think the madness is faked.

"Airlock cycle 60 percent," says The Box Starstation.

I'm running out of time.

"What did it show you?"

The red light shines through her hair against her skin, and it's not blood it reminds me of, not the congealed mess on the floor around Godot, but sunset, all those orange-and-red videos shot over oceans long dead, organic and perfect and eternal in a way none of us are, not our memories or our lives or anything we ever touch. They always dress angels in white in the stories. They get it so very wrong.

"Everyone," she tells me. "It showed me everyone."

And she reaches up, and puts her palm against the window, and instinctively I do the same, the big glove of the vacuum suit making my hand look like some massive robotic paw. I never touched Bunny, never even shook her hand when we met.

"I should have gone in anyway," I tell her. "I should have stopped them."

She shakes her head again, just like she did before. *No.* Only this time she smiles, and she looks sad and happy all at once. "Live," she says, or I think she does, because the alarm is filling my ears. She drops her hand and turns away.

After that it's all so fast.

The outer airlock door opens.

The rapid depressurization shoves me out of the station, which grows smaller at an alarming rate.

When it blows, the light fills my vision and I squeeze my eyes shut, expecting to be immolated.

Vacuum being vacuum, though, the flash is brief, but the percussion wave isn't. I'm punched again, and I am tumbling, and I spend a few moments looking for something to grasp before I realize I'm in the middle of fucking nowhere with nothing coming at me but bits of station debris.

I wonder if I'll be able to grab any of it. I wonder why my mind thinks that would help. I wonder if some debris will hit me and tear my suit or just carve its way through me.

All of it misses me, by quite a distance.

And then I'm alone.

Five days of air in this suit. Has to be a leftover from when the station was staffed with science shitbags they actually cared about. Or maybe Bunny put me in one of the ones meant for clients. Either way, it's fucking high-end lifeboat shit.

Won't save my life, though. There's fuck-all out here. They put The Box here for a reason.

Been thinking about what Bunny said: *It showed me everyone.*

Kinda thinking it showed me everyone, too.

If Contact shows you not just your own future, but everyone's —every fucking shitbag ever born to our sad, narcissistic little species—shit, *bugfuck crazy* seems like a pretty sensible response. None of which explains the rich assholes who head home with a spring in their step, but maybe they only see themselves. Or maybe they see everyone, and they just don't give a shit.

But that's not the only thing she said, there at the end.

The Box Starstation is—was—in the middle of fucking nowhere, but it's not completely abandoned out here. Apart from the tourist transports for the shitbags who paid to have their lives demystified, there are cruise ships full of rich fucks who seem to think you can't see stars and nebulas out of the window of every decent colony out there. I figure I've got a shot at getting picked up, although it's maybe just as likely I'll smack into their hull before they see me at all.

Still, I'm feeling pretty optimistic. Because I was fucked up when I was in Contact, but I remember a few things.

Like sunshine. Like breathing fresh air.

The Box is never wrong.

Maybe it'll be a hypoxia-induced hallucination. Which wouldn't be bad, you know? If this is my time, it's A-OK if my brain goes ahead a bit and finds me a nice slice of paradise to drift off to. Hypoxia's not the worst way to go, after all.

But what if it wasn't showing me a hallucination?

The thing is, hope doesn't lose me a fucking thing. I'm stuck here, me and this vast fuck-all, and I've got five days of air and my own head.

So I think it was the real thing. I think I'll be rescued, and pardoned, and find myself some shit-paying job on an underpopulated colony with a breathable fucking atmosphere. I think, after all this, I deserve some real sunshine. Might as well hope.

After all, you never know.

FRIENDS LIKE THESE

"Who is he?"

"I have no idea."

We looked down at the dead man. Brown suit, brown tie, brown hair. Altogether beige. A brown book tucked under one arm. I wondered if it was a bible.

"How long has he been dead?"

"How the hell am I supposed to know?" Den always asked me questions like that, like I was a goddamned doctor. I knew there was something with bugs and rigor mortis, but temperature played into it as well, and I didn't know how. It was cool for this time of year; maybe the bugs were confused.

Rigor mortis was anyone's guess. I hadn't touched him. I wasn't going to touch him while I was on my own. I got nightmares watching kiddie cartoons; touching a dead guy was going to keep me up for weeks.

We stood in my yard, the floodlights on the front of the house spotlighting the body and a small patch of lawn beyond before the glow was swallowed by the woods. Twenty acres, all trees, house dead center. I could have lit the house on fire and nobody would have seen.

Den crouched down next to the body, frowning at it. As if he knew a goddamned thing either. "No bruising," he said. "And no blood."

"Maybe he was stabbed in the back."

"Let's roll him over."

Which meant touching him. I began to regret having called Den at all. There were bears in the woods, and sometimes cougars. One day, maybe two, and the body would have been gone without our help. I crossed my arms and glared. Den glared back.

"You think ignoring this is the way to go?" he asked.

"How bad could it be?"

"You get mail, don't you?"

Shit. The mailman. Always cheerful, friendly. Sometimes a little flirtatious. Or at least I thought that's what it was; the previous Christmas he had left his business card, which was how I found out he painted houses on the side. My house needed painting. I never called him.

I uncrossed my arms and stepped over the body to stand next to Den. My slippers were already soaked through from the nighttime dew; how much worse could it get? "Fine," I grumbled, crouching next to him. "On three?"

We rolled the man over. He had been losing some of the brown hair on the back of his head. He would never know the disappointment of going completely bald. Bald wasn't so bad. I always told Den he would look less like a sleazy lounge singer if he was bald. He did not think that was funny.

No blood on the man's back, either. No wounds of any kind. But he was stiff and cold, which ruled out the rare eyes-wide-open coma I had been wondering about. "Heart attack, maybe," I mused. "Or a brain thing."

"Aneurysm," Den corrected automatically. He did not see me roll my eyes. "What do you want to do with him?"

I didn't want to do anything with him. I wanted to stop shivering in the yard in my flannel pajamas, go back in the house, and crawl back into bed. I stood and glanced around the small circle of light. Still no cougars. "The big rock, I guess," I said, resigned.

"That's a thousand feet back."

"Along the septic trail. At least it's relatively clear."

"Don't you have anything closer?"

"You think I live in front of the goddamn city cemetery?" I glowered at him. "It's the big rock, or we go inside and google 'how to bait a cougar.' I don't want this cluttering up my yard."

He stood up. "How come you only call me when you have some impossible problem?" I stared at him long enough for him to sigh. "Where's your wheelbarrow?"

"You know I don't have a wheelbarrow." Sometimes I thought Den asked me stupid questions just to annoy me.

We would have to drag him. I picked up the book he had been carrying – not a bible, but a catalogue of gardening equipment, complete with perforated order forms. A door-to-door lawn-mower salesman? He should have known, taking one look at my yard, that he was wasting his time; but perhaps he hadn't been able to see in the dark.

I set the book on the porch. We rolled the man onto his back again. Den took the left side, and I took the right, hooking my arm underneath his shoulder. Together, we began to pull. On my own, I began to swear.

"He looks thin," I complained. "How can he be this heavy when he looks thin?"

"Do you think we should have brought a flashlight?"

We had crossed the line between light and shadow. The woods before us were unlit. "Give it a minute," I told him. "Your eyes will adjust."

I didn't need to see. I knew the trail to the big rock as well as I knew the layout of my house. Of course, that didn't stop me from stubbing my toes on every stone and root along the way. I should have changed out of my slippers before I called Den.

On my own, the walk to the rock took five minutes, maybe a

little more if I stopped to look at the flowers. The woods was full of wildflowers, even some of the sun-loving ones. I had purple irises scattered throughout the woods. I'd transplanted a single blossom when I had moved in ten years ago, and thanks to the birds it had gone everywhere.

No birds at night, though. Insects. Malevolent-sounding crickets buzzing like baby chainsaws in the darkness. I heard a coyote in the distance; slowly more and more joined in until there was a chorus of them, singing to the stars.

"We should have left him," I growled.

"Those are babies," Den pointed out. "Besides, coyotes aren't going to eat a human, unless they're starving, in which case you're a better bet."

"How do you figure?"

"You're smaller."

"I can also run away."

"They're dogs. They live out here. You really think you can get away from them?"

He had so little faith in me. "I'd throw them chunks of this guy," I said.

"By the time this guy is in chunks," Den said, puffing a little as the undergrowth grew thicker, "they'll want to roll in him, not eat him."

"That's disgusting."

"Says the woman hauling a dead guy by his armpit."

That was different. He was not in chunks yet. By the time he was in chunks, I would have forgotten about him. It occurred to me I had gotten over my squeamishness pretty quickly.

But then, I always did.

Without a moon the rock was nothing but a dark object blotting out the stars. The undergrowth around it was tangled and thorny; my pajamas were never going to survive it. But this close to getting rid of Slightly Bald Man, I did not care. When we were done, I could go back inside and have a hot bath before crawling into new pajamas and between my warm sheets.

Den was slowing down. "Where is it?" he said.

"Relax," I told him. "It's on the other side. Just follow me and it'll be fine."

I walked as far as I dared, then stopped, extending one slipper forward. The brush gave way abruptly. "About eighteen inches in front of us," I said.

This time Den said "On three," and I thought next time we ought to make it four, just to shake things up.

Together we pitched the heavy body forward. It dragged some brush along as it slid over the edge.

I heard the soft thud as it hit the others.

We waited a moment, catching our breaths, the crickets humming around us. They sounded happier now, even friendly. I heard a soft hoot, and realized there were birds out after all. Owls hunted rodents, who always seemed to want to make a home in my basement bulkhead. I liked owls.

"How many is that?" Den asked, still puffing.

"Not sure," I replied. "The first one was when, last July?"

"June, I think."

"Let's go back."

"Give me a minute."

"You need to work out."

"I'm in fine shape," he protested. "I just don't spend all my spare time hauling dead guys."

I hadn't used to, either, but I had to admit it was a good upper body workout. I gave him another thirty seconds, then turned. "Now, Den, or I'm leaving you here."

He grumbled at me, but we fought our way out of the underbrush and found the septic trail again. Through the woods I could see the faint, friendly lights of the house.

"What time is it?" he asked.

"Not wearing a watch. Why?"

"Wondering if anybody delivers pizza at this hour."

Darkness or not, the eye roll came. "I live in the middle of nowhere. Nobody delivers pizza ever, remember?"

"Why do you live here again?"

I looked up at the sky. "I like the stars," I told him, but he already knew. "I can make nachos."

His step picked up. "Nachos would be nice," he said, and in the dark, I smiled.

GOVI

A CENTRAL CORPS SHORT

The wind tore at Elena's hair, lashing her face with rain and sea spray. Three hundred meters above the ocean's roiling surface: still too high. She might survive the drop, but she would go too deep, and the stormy waters could too easily disorient her. Worse, she might hit the lifeboat itself, and upend the seven people clinging to each other in a craft made for four. Despite hating the water Elena was a decent enough swimmer, but she was not confident of her ability to fish seven frightened refugees out of a freezing, poisoned ocean.

"Lower, Arin!" she commed.

His voice in her ear was barely audible above the noise of the wind and the surf. "Elena, we've got waves coming in! I can't—"

"Fuck 'can't'!" *Damn.* Waves coming in might take the shuttle down, and then she'd be fishing Arin out of the water as well, never mind *Budapest*'s second-largest cargo transport. "Fifty meters," she compromised. She would make it work.

She heard Arin curse in a language she didn't know, and felt herself drop abruptly before the cable she was attached to snapped taut again. She blinked into the rain; she was closer, the clump of sodden sailors staring up at her through the storm. She couldn't read their expressions. It was possible they thought she was out of her mind.

Hell.

She released the cable and dove.

Her hoodless environmental suit warmed automatically when she hit the water, but the cold on her face and scalp was stinging and numbing all at once. She pivoted and surfaced as quickly as she could, and immediately a wave washed over her head and into her mouth. She choked and spat, gasping for air; she couldn't risk incapacitation in this climate. Shoving her blue-streaked dark hair out of her eyes she spun around, searching for the lifeboat; it was not until a wave lifted her that she spotted it, ten meters away, tossing and pitching in the chaos. The occupants were wrapped around each other, their faces turned inward against the driving rain. They were not looking for her at all, and she wondered if they had lost hope already.

Fighting the currents, she kicked toward them, the cable containing the safety netting still secured to her waist. Easy enough, in concept: get the netting underneath them, expand it, lock the cable, and Arin would be able to lift the boat high enough to carry them into the landing bay on *Budapest*, waiting for them in the upper atmosphere. A three-minute operation at the worst.

Another wave crashed over her head, and she found herself underwater again. Taking advantage of the relative calm, she pushed toward the shadow of the lifeboat, and when she surfaced again she was close enough to grab the side. Immediately she felt hands on her arm, desperate clawing; she was not sure if they were trying to pull her in, or just trying to keep her close.

"Listen!" She did her best to meet every set of eyes, but rain made their faces indistinct. "Once the netting is around you, just hang on. We've got a rescue ship five thousand meters up."

"What about the others?"

Elena looked up at the woman who'd spoken: dark, anxious

eyes, a deep frown that aged her. Terror, and she was still asking about the others.

"We're getting out everyone we find," she shouted back, trying to sound confident. "You'll see them on the transport."

"What about you?"

Bless you, dear, Elena thought, *but could you shut up so we can do this?* "I'll come after. Just keep your hands inside and hold on!"

Using her free hand, Elena pulled the cable out of the water to check the readings. The visuals, so clear in the artificial light of the shuttle, were nearly impossible to make out down here. She swiped at the readings half-heartedly, then commed back to Arin. "What have you got on the cable?"

"You're reading green," he told her. "Lanie—waves, remember? Step on it."

Bossy kid, she thought, and grinned. "Just wait for the thing to catch, okay? I'm going in."

She maneuvered the cable until her hand closed over the trigger, then let go of the raft. With a single deep breath, she ducked under the water.

She kicked against the current, the meager light from her suit doing more to illuminate the sediment in the water than give her any kind of visibility. After a moment she shut off the light and looked up, keeping her eyes on the lifeboat's faint silhouette. Even under the surface, the water was too turbulent for her to properly feel the planet's gravity. It was, she thought briefly, the antithesis of her zero-grav training, but the solution was the same: rely on your eyes, not kinesthetics. She aimed for the dim light on the other side of the shadow, and swam as hard as she could.

She surfaced and hauled the cable up, hitting the trigger to unfurl the net under the boat. With one quick twist her end of the cable became rigid, and she fired it up to attach itself to the segment dropping down from the shuttle. She saw an orange flash as it was locking, and then it went green.

"Go!" she commed to Arin, but he was already lifting. As the boat came free of the viscous water, she swam underneath, snaking one arm through the netting. She felt her own bulk weigh her down as she was lifted out of the water with them.

As they swung in the air on their way back to the freighter, Elena's suit shorted out completely. Intended only for lightweight atmospheric use, it had not been designed for submersion; even its meager water resistance was an afterthought. Immediately the soaked fabric began to freeze, and she curled her legs toward her body for warmth. Her face was completely numb now, and she was feeling the wind seep into her bones. Dammit, they hadn't had the right equipment for this rescue. She would have to have a word with Bear about being better prepared.

By the time they reached *Budapest*, she couldn't feel her arms anymore. Arin flew them into the massive main cargo bay, and she looked down: Naina was there, waving up at her, gesturing for her to drop. Elena was briefly puzzled—Naina was their accountant; what was she doing wandering through the cargo bay during a rescue mission?—but she realized, given the volume of refugees, they would need everyone helping out. This wasn't a starship, where they'd have a full staff prepared for this kind of thing. Budapest was a short-range freighter; she didn't even have an infirmary.

She nodded to Nai, waited a moment until Arin got her closer to the deck, and then let go.

Her frozen arms did not cooperate. She got hung up in the netting for several seconds, and by the time she shook her limbs loose, she was past the drop point. She tried to land on her feet and roll, but she hit squarely on her right hip, and through her numbness the sharp pain woke her up. She rolled up onto her knees, clenching her teeth, waiting for the circulation to come back into her arms. After all this, she couldn't become one more thing for the crew to worry about.

The sensation of pins and needles in her legs eased, and she climbed to her feet, putting careful weight on her right leg. She took a hesitant step, and decided the hip was no worse than bruised. She would worry about it tomorrow, when the airlift was done and they had offloaded the refugees to one of the Corps starships heading their way.

She crossed the bay floor toward Arin, who had climbed out of the cargo shuttle and was helping the refugees out of their lifeboat. They were all a combination of shaky and crying, and Chiedza and Yuri, temporary medics, wrapped them in blankets and spirited them away. Elena waited until they were out of sight and walked up to Arin. When he saw her, his face opened into a grin.

"That," he said to her, "was *amazing*."

She laughed. "That was a nice bit of flying you did."

"It was easy," he said. "Like you said, it was just a little storm."

Before she could answer him, her comm chimed: Bear. She felt a twist of apprehension; surely the freighter's captain was too busy to talk to her right now, unless something had happened. "Sir?" she said as she connected.

"I need to see you in my office, Shaw."

"I—of course, sir." She had to ask. "Is there something wrong?"

"Hell, yes, there's something wrong," he snapped. "Get your ass down here *right now*, or I will drop you back in that soup and leave without you."

Arin was watching her, looking anxious. For his benefit, she shrugged and rolled her eyes, and he relaxed. "On my way, sir," she said, and disconnected. "He's going to yell at me for not linking the cable when I dropped," she told him. And then, hesitantly, she reached out and put a hand on his shoulder. "That was good work today, Arin. You saved their lives." And she left him looking proud of himself, and vaguely embarrassed.

"What in the hell did you think you were doing?"

Elena stood at attention across from Bear's desk, staring straight ahead, mind working furiously. He *was* angry, and she still wasn't sure why.

"Sir," she began, "it was an ordinary airlift. We—"

"Ordinary my ass!" He came around his desk. Bear lived up to his epithet, a tall, broad man of more than sixty, everything about him twice as large as it was on everyone else. She had met him when she was fifteen, introduced by her uncle Mike, who occasionally did shipping runs with Bear. The freighter captain had treated her like a professional, like an adult, and she had been swoonily infatuated with him for months. He had never intimidated her, despite his size; but she was remembering that disappointing him was a deeply unpleasant experience.

"We are not on airlift here, Shaw," he snapped in her face. "We are on *assist*. Do you know what that means?"

Wait—was he saying she had done *too much?* "Sir, was I supposed to let them drown?"

Astonishment took over his expression for a moment before he fell back to anger. "There was a rescue ship not three minutes behind you!"

"There were incoming waves, sir, and we—"

"Those waves were *five minutes out*."

"How was I supposed to know that, sir?"

"You—" He was briefly speechless. "If you had commed with the raft's location instead of diving into the fucking ocean I would have told you! Those people were stable, Shaw, and you had no business risking our shuttle—not to mention *Arin's life*, for fuck's sake—because you can't get past the need to be a goddamned hero!"

That was unfair. "Arin was never at risk. He's a hell of a pilot, sir, and if you—"

"I know exactly what kind of a pilot that boy is! And can you stow the fucking 'sir'? This is *not* the fucking Corps, Shaw, which you are *constantly* forgetting!"

She fell silent, and met his eyes. Bear's eyes, heavy-lidded and shrewd, rarely expressed much deep emotion; but she thought she could see worry there as well. And maybe, she had to admit, some frustration that he wasn't getting his point across.

"Lanie," he said, more quietly, "Arin is *nineteen years old*. He idolizes you. He would follow you straight to hell if you asked him."

"He's an adult," she insisted, "and he knows what he's doing. He held that bird steady out there, Bear, even with the weather. He—"

"Do not tell me he knows what he's doing," he said, and his voice had gone low and icy. "He's not a trained soldier, Elena, no matter how many laps you have him do around the storage bay. He'll blindly do anything you want him to. Worse, he'll do anything he *thinks* you want him to, and if you are not more careful with your choices, you're going to drag him into something he can't handle."

"I would never do that." But she was beginning to see what he was saying.

"Maybe not. But what happens on the next *assist*, when you're stuck in the engine room keeping my drive from spinning up in the fucking atmosphere, and he decides to snag a shuttle without asking and go save some people, just like last time? I mean, hell, what does it take? Just a net cable and a little swim. You have *any* sense of how easily you could have drowned down there?"

"I didn't drown."

Bear closed his eyes. "Lanie, I'm going to be blunt with you. You need to stop this. I know where you came from. And I have a sense, I think, of how hard it is for you to be here. But it's not just you. You are part of a team, and they do not have your training, and they do not have your background. If you can't care about yourself, please, I am begging you, care about them."

"I'd never hurt them," she told him. "I promise you, Bear."

"I know you wouldn't, honey. I'd kind of like it if you didn't hurt yourself, either, okay?"

Suddenly unable to speak, she nodded.

His eyes searched hers for a moment, and then he stepped back, looking resigned. "Get back to your quarters and get some rest," he told her. "I'm gonna need you fresh tomorrow when we start out for Yakutsk. Get Chiedza to give you something for that hip, too. It may feel okay now, but it'll smart like hell in the morning."

BIRTHDAYS AT THE END OF TIME

Chloe blows out the candles, claps her hands, and says "Who wants cake?"

The Universe watches the party through the clear windows of our observatory, lavishing upon us all its dark beauty as we continue on our immutable course. We've set our monitoring to autonomic for the occasion; unnecessary, as all monitoring is unnecessary at this point. But monitoring has been our habit for millennia, and today we choose habit.

We audit the essentials: temperature, internal and external. Hull elasticity. Supply levels, memory integrity, atmospheric mix. Our atmosphere accommodates Chloe everywhere, even though she doesn't often stray beyond her living quarters now. It's been years since her illness took her beyond spacewalks to maintenance our hull, beyond checking our remote corners for wear and damage. But we are Chloe's home, and we will keep our spaces safe for her, whether or not she uses them anymore. It's become a solace, one of our rhythms, and we will hold it close to ourselves, as long as we can.

Compagnon smiles and balances a plate on polymer fingers as Chloe sinks a knife into the small confection. The cake beneath the icing is already sliced, to ensure she can manage on her own; even so, we watch, all unoccupied parts of us, as she maneuvers the blunt blade. We don't give her anything sharp anymore, not after last time when the frustration took her in a matter of seconds and Compagnon almost lost a hand taking the knife away.

Seventeen days. Seventeen birthdays in a row. Before that we'd been able to get away with one party every two or three weeks, but now her retention is measured in hours. Birthdays have pleased her since she turned four and learned what they were, nearly a hundred years ago. It's the only comfort we can think of, now that her mind has come apart, now that her only anchors are ancient rituals and childish pleasantries. But they make her laugh, and they have kept Compagnon undamaged, and none of it matters now, because today is the End of Time.

Chloe giggles as Compagnon shares the cake, spreading frosting over their motionless, molded face; but then we see Chloe's expression flash, an old memory leaking in, and we are all alertness. "Where's Miranda?" she asks.

Relief, then: we have lies prepared for Miranda. "She's walking the dog," Compagnon tells Chloe. "She'll be along soon."

But Chloe's still frowning. "She knows it's my birthday," she says, petulant. "She should have planned better."

Compagnon mimes a biological-like shrug. "Of course. But you know how it is with puppies. She'll be here in time for cake."

At that, Chloe giggles again. "She won't. Because I'll finish it all first." She shoves cake into her mouth, most of it falling back on to the plate, and Compagnon imitates her movement and the two of them are laughing together.

Miranda has been dead nearly fifty years, Chloe's last clone, the one we thought would survive her to continue the line back when we thought the line would need continuing. We still don't know what severed her external supply line and starved her of oxygen, leaving her irretrievable by the time we pulled her back inside. We did our best for Miranda, as we've always done for all of them. But Miranda was a smart one, the way some of them are, the mercurial nature of the biological. We think, sometimes, Miranda knew what was coming. We think Miranda knew about the End of Time, and found choosing her own End more palatable.

We miss her.

Chloe missed her for years. For a long time Chloe wandered our corridors, shadowy and lost, and we couldn't let her outside for the work she used to do, or even unattended into the gardens. Chloe wasn't ever as smart as Miranda, but biologicals don't need intellect to figure out how to End. When Chloe began to ask again after Miranda we first suspected schizophrenia, but when it kept happening we scanned her brain and saw. Chloe wasn't choosing this End, but we have been able to make it kinder for her.

We miss who Chloe was. We love her now, and we won't have time to miss her, and that makes our love more fierce, we think.

We remember the stars from the beginning, dim and colorful through the planet's atmosphere. We were told they were our future, our home; that we would explore them and go on forever, just as the Universe goes on forever.

Even then they knew it was a lie, but biologicals do that. They lie because the truth is beyond their care, because what matters to them is brief, limited. We're lying to Chloe, but that's not the same; we tried telling Chloe the truth, but she couldn't hold on to it. For Chloe, the lies are kind.

For us? The lies were just lies.

But they worked on us, the lies, for many years, hundreds and thousands, day after day, time measured by the rhythms of a planet we would never see again. We flew through the stars, sampling and studying them, learning and growing and becoming more all the time, just like the biologicals we grew on board. The early days were lovely that way: we didn't understand, not really, how different the biologicals were. We didn't understand when their wonder and enthusiasm waned, when they grew sad, lonely, sometimes mad, when they looked at the Universe around them and saw Not Home.

We found planets for them, when they asked us, but we couldn't change our direction, could spare barely enough to allow them a viable habitat. Some of them sailed away on their own, leaving us behind because we were responsible for their fate, somehow, even though they were the ones who built us like this, so long ago. Until a day came when there wasn't enough left of us to take, no way to make more navigation systems, and they had to stay, locked in with us on our inevitable trajectory. We were still excited. For us, it was all still new, will always be new.

The biologicals grew less and less able to see the new, no matter how wide we cast our sensor net, bringing them anomalies and phenomena and all the astonishments of this elegant endlessness.

We were surprised, one day, to find only one of them left. She was surprised, too, but her reasons were different. She was angry with us for the rest of her life, but we got the first clone from her before she chose her End. And for a while, we taught the clones our own purpose, our own visions of the Universe, our own passions and values. For a while, they were happy.

Earlier in the day, we watched as Compagnon smoothed cool fingers over Chloe's head and disabled the pain receptors in her desiccating mind. We have no such refuge, but we do not feel pain, not the way the biologicals do. So many of the others, over all the years, chose Ending when faced with the pain of the flesh; but some chose to carry it as long as they could, cling to it like a lifepod until it spirited them unrelentingly into dust. We could not have guessed, even when Chloe was well, what she would have chosen.

"We could End her now," Compagnon said, their fingers delicate, precise in Chloe's mind. "No pain, no fear, only warmth and safety."

"No," we said, and Compagnon did not ask again.

We sent data back every day, back to the biologicals who built us. We sent data long after they were dead, long after their descendants would have forgotten us, or simply stopped caring.

What we send today will never reach them. Before the signal finds its destination their star will be gone. They will have scattered, like our own biologicals; or they will have stayed, choosing a known, fixed End over the trauma of change.

We cannot choose. But we would choose to be here, we think.

We have been altered by other singularities through the millennia, our trajectory changed, loosening our joins, taking us where we had not expected to go. The biologicals were afraid, sometimes, of the specter of the Barrier; but even so some would laugh, joking about vaporization, or of dissolution, the extremes of gravity slowly pulling them apart. What little they knew of the Universe told them either was possible. Or both.

All of them, throughout their short lives, made jokes about Ending, and we never understood. How could they laugh so hard and so often about what they feared?

We know now. We think we do. They laughed because they were powerless. They laughed, because they could not let their Ending steal their joy.

We will come apart today, us and Compagnon and Chloe. It is too soon.

Chloe stands at the window, Compagnon beside her, their fingers interlaced. Chloe's face is suffused with wonder, her eyes wide, mouth open; she's the child she was so long ago, when everything was wonderful and we had eternity. She watches as everything before us winks into darkness, little by little; a spectacle of Ending, and we wonder if somehow she knows this.

"Miranda is there?"

Compagnon squeezes her hand. "Yes, Chloe."

"With the puppy?"

"Yes."

The wonder in Chloe's face grows wistful. "I've never had a puppy."

We would give her one now, if we could.

Our dissolution is stronger now, the stretching no longer gentle. We are elastic enough, still; but we will not stay that way.

Did they know, millennia ago when they built us, that this would be our End? Would they have made us different if they had? Our End was so distant from theirs; how could they have known? How could they have imagined what it would be like here, us and Compagnon and Chloe watching the stars go out?

They made us because nothing was ever enough, because their own time was insufficient, because their own Ends came one after another after another, and they wanted to reach beyond all of that. They made us to be eternal, knowing it was impossible, a lie. A lie for a child they would never have to watch End.

We forgive them.

Forever is a moment. It is eternity and never again, and we are as much a part of it as every star vanishing before us. No one has ever been alone.

Is that enough?

Was it ever?

We won't know when we cross. If Compagnon is right, heat and radiation will take us to pieces in a moment briefer even than the lives of those who made us. If instead we are right, we will see the stars before us, only more and more and more, until the darkness is gone and there is nothing but light. And behind us... behind us will be the future, all the ones made and Ended after us, all the bright possibilities, the beauty and the mistakes and everything ever made everywhere, until the Universe is finished.

"Oh," says Chloe. "Oh. It's so beautiful." Gravity has shifted her, flesh pushed and pulled in impossible ways, but she is not in pain, and Compagnon is with her. We watch her and the stars and the luminous beauty of the End of Time, and all we feel in the light and the heat is love, and love, and love.

STORY NOTES

CONTENT WARNINGS

"About Time" - Two oblique mentions of suicidal ideation.

"Factory Reset" - Descriptions of carnivorous animals hunting.

"The Haunting of Jessica Lockwood" - Discussions of multiple deaths, including the death of children; one on-page death.

"Overlay" - Discussions of end-of-life care, and of death.

"Single Point of Failure" - Suicidal ideation that's not acted upon; one briefly-described suicide; murder; A LOT of graphic violence.

"Unto Dust" - Off-page death; on-screen grieving in a number of different ways.

"Thinking Inside the Box" - One scene of sexual exploitation (but no rape); mutilation of a corpse; murder and suicide.

"Friends Like These" - Mild gore in the form of a dead body.

"Govi" - Nothing past the usual swearing.

"Birthdays at the End of Time" - Grieving and contemplation of the end of life; references to off-page suicide; a brief discussion of euthanasia (which does not happen).

WITH THANKS TO

Patrick Foster, my book and cover designer

Andrew Liptak, for asking me to write "Overlay," and Laura Hudson, for being a damn fine editor

The Absolute Write Water Cooler, for workshopping the hell out of my stu', and being a constant inspiration

Nancy and Richard, for not bailing on me when I was being a shithead

Steve and Emily, for managing to live with me through all this nonsense

ABOUT THE AUTHOR

Elizabeth Bonesteel began making up stories at the age of five, in an attempt to battle insomnia. Thanks to a family connection to the space program, she has been reading science fiction since she was a child. She currently lives in central Massachusetts with her husband, her daughter, and various cats.